HARVEST AMERICAN
Writing

TALLER WOMEN

OTHER BOOKS BY LAWRENCE NAUMOFF

The Night of the Weeping Women

Rootie Kazootie

Lawrence Naumoff

TALLER WOMEN

A Cautionary Tale

A Harvest Book

Harcourt Brace & Company

SAN DIEGO   NEW YORK   LONDON

To Marianne Gingher,
with all my love and respect.

Library of Congress Cataloging-in-Publication Data
Naumoff, Lawrence.
Taller women: a cautionary tale/Lawrence Naumoff.—1st ed.
p.   cm.
ISBN 0-15-187991-5
ISBN 0-15-688162-4 (pbk.)
I. Title.
PS3564.A8745T3   1992
813'.54—dc20   92-1312

Designed by Trina Stahl

Printed in the United States of America

First Harvest edition 1994

A B C D E

To the following people I give my heartfelt thanks for their support or friendship or shared vision, over the years.

Alane Mason and Max Steele and Reynolds Price and Leon Rooke and Carolyn Kizer and Morgan Entrekin and Daphne Athas and Sylvia Wilkinson and Linda Healey and Kathy Banks and Doris Betts and Jessie Rehder (gone but never forgotten) and Barbara Lowenstein and in the state of Maine of mind, Carolyn Chute, and in England, Andy McKillop.

The Whiting Foundation.

My son Michael, for being who you are: true, honest, brave, and ever do I learn from you.

TALLER WOMEN

AT THE MOMENT MONROE was ready to unlock his front door, the girl next door called to him, and then fell in the grass, and a dog, coming from down the street, turned around, and went home.

Had the girl not yelled, Monroe would not have noticed her, because he had been lost in thought about how nice it would be to live with a woman who did not later turn out to be crazy, or sad, or depressed, or desperate, and in the middle of this, he saw the girl's legs fold up in the same helpless way his had when Lydia threw the rock at him.

The rock had been on the table. He had found it in the woods. It was weathered, and resembled the head of a Mayan god, and it was one of the early presents he'd given Lydia when they began living together. She loved this rock.

When she threw it, and struck him at the top of his spine, he dropped immediately, like a puppet whose strings had been severed, which was the same way the girl next door fell.

Between Monroe and the girl was a hedge, and

along this hedge, honeysuckle vines grew. It was spring, and the blooms were covered with bees, buzzing and hovering.

There was a break in this hedge, and Monroe ran to the girl, who was in her late teens, and wore shorts, a flannel shirt, and cowboy boots. The clothes were ragged, and her hair was uncombed, and she looked wild, and feral, as if she'd been raised by wolves.

Her eyes were open, and her pupils were green, deep green, an unusually deep, emerald green, and the whites, or sclera, were pure and clean.

This is a healthy girl, Monroe thought, at least from the appearance of her eyes.

"Do you need help?" he asked.

She rolled onto her back, and smiled, and then rolled away from him, and then back again, and she did this effortlessly, and innocently, but it did not look innocent to Monroe.

It looked like the way Katy, his ex-wife, used to roll back and forth in bed when she was aroused, torquing this way and that, first toward him, and then away, as if she were trying to escape from him, and what she was feeling, but had to roll back, to get more.

Then Monroe heard a bell, like a ship's bell, ringing from behind the girl's house, and the girl sprang up, and ran. He marveled at her leap onto the porch, and then he left her yard, and passed through the break in the hedge, and the bees swarmed around him.

WHILE THE BEES swarmed, people all over town were leaving work for home.

An old man left a narrow brick building, and the old man was Ronnie's father, and Ronnie was the girl who'd fallen in the grass. Inside the house, toward which the old man would slowly drive, his young daughter was fleeing from her enormous mother.

Ronnie was safe, though, because she could run like a deer, and when she leapt the back of the couch like a hurdler over the crossbar of a jump, her mother hit the back of the couch and tumbled forward. She made a good recovery, however, and continued after her, and the chase went on and on and on. When the old man finally did arrive, and entered the house, he got knocked into the wall and then slammed, along with the door, the other way, and he ended up once more on the porch, on his hands and knees, like a well-dressed bum who'd been kicked into the gutter.

About the same time, Lydia, who'd thrown the rock a year earlier at Monroe, left the hospital on her way home, too, but was stuck in traffic, and about out of gas. The needle dropped. She thought, now I'll never make it and I won't have time to see Martha, and she cursed the gridlock that gripped her car.

GRIDLOCK, TIGHT AS a man's hand around a slender neck, was a function of life these days, as people were forced to learn how to breathe differently, in short, hard gasps, and then to draw in all they would need until the next time.

Breathing had become conscious, making life that much more difficult, as the sympathetic nervous system lost its sympathy and the autonomic controls of innervation surrendered. Doctors in emergency rooms cocked their heads to one side like animals in the forest hearing strange sounds, new sounds, and they stepped quietly from room to room, wondering at this self-possession that had altered diaphragms.

Iron lungs were brought out of storage, and mirrors were set up above the people so they could see what they'd done to themselves, and what they now looked like, physiologic deviations of excited neuritis.

Sedatives were called for. Fixations of tissues to prevent movement, and the application of heat, glaring lights and educated hands trailing up and down the numbed torsos, all had the doctors peering out the windows and down the halls to see who, and what, was next.

Like Lydia, they had all read about the court case in California involving freedom of religion, where a man, inventing his own religion with one thousand members, argued his own defense, and told of a force moving through him, which he described as over-whelming, and which spoke to him, and told him that his wife, to become a high priestess, had to accept the sacrifice of the thousand men, and along with the sacrifice, a donation of one hundred dollars.

His wife had fulfilled the requirements, and was then allowed the benefits of priesthood, and at the age of forty-seven, found herself equal to her husband, but with some difficulty in breathing.

Then, just at that moment, late in the day, when no one thought they would ever get home, that the day would never end, that nothing would ever be right again, the gridlock broke, and the traffic moved, and Ronnie outran her mother, and her father crawled in off the porch, and Lydia made it to a gas station, and Monroe sat quietly, and the dog that had started across the lawn, where Ronnie had fallen, came out from under the porch, and went through the break in the hedge, and down the street, avoiding Lydia's car, as it slid around a curve below her house, and the dog sniffed the air behind the car, and sneezed.

The dog was on its way to a meeting. All the animals in the neighborhood were getting together.

"I ALMOST HIT that dog," Lydia said, jumping out of her car. "I've almost hit a bunch of them lately. Cats, too."

"Slow down, then," Monroe told her.

"I'm going as slow as I can."

"I guess you are."

"I'm sorry I'm late, by the way."

"That's all right."

He looked at the rag hanging out of her gas tank. It looked like a fuse, and the old car took on the resemblance of a Molotov cocktail, on wheels.

"Lost your cap again?" he asked.

"Sure. I did. I surely did. Darn it."

"They make a gas cap with a chain on it," he said.

"I need that," she said. "Find me one of those."

"Of course, they are also inventing an electric car."

"Get me one, then," she said.

"But you have to remember to plug it in, at night."

"Then I'm lucky to have a fellow like you around to remind me," she said. "I'm sure lucky about that."

"Yes," he said. "You are."

"I'm late because I went to see Martha. We had a long talk. I can't tell you what about."

"Okay."

"I want to, but I promised."

"Don't, then."

"I suppose people tell husbands and wives things they don't tell anyone else, and it's almost like we're married, but I promised I wouldn't."

"Then, don't."

"But I want to."

"Well, do, then."

"But I can't."

It was important to talk. When the talk stopped, the gestures of the open hand changed, and fists formed, and rigid jaws fractured like glass, and old men shook, and young girls raced about town, and people began chasing one another, not knowing why, just wanting to catch someone and make them talk, make them tell, make them give, make them be still.

"THIS HAS GOT to stop," old Mr. Cutler, next door, on his knees, said, echoing what everyone else was thinking.

Ronnie saw him, crawling down the hall.

"Got to stop," he said again, gasping it out.

His wife, Ronnie's mother, the enormous Mrs. Cutler, the woman of the house, was also on her hands and knees, in the kitchen, leaning over a glass of water.

"It's her fault," she said.

"It's not mine," Ronnie told them both.

Ronnie had brought her mother the water, and gotten a glass for herself, and when she saw her father crawling toward her, she helped him into a chair, and got him one, too. His hands trembled. She steadied the glass. She helped him drink.

"I wish you'd go somewhere," her mother said.

"Yeah," Ronnie said, "like I don't, huh?"

"I wish you'd do something with yourself," she said.

"I wish you'd do something with yourself, too," Ronnie said, "like die, or something."

"Cute. Real cute."

"Now Veronica," her father said. "You know we both love you."

"Quite," Ronnie said. "Quite so, indeed."

"I STILL HAVE my headache," Lydia said.

"Do you need some aspirin?"

"No, but look where I'm pointing. See this spot? What kind of headache would that be, from what you know about them?"

"It could be anything," he said.

"Put your finger there. Can you feel it throbbing?"

"No."

"But why?"

"It's too faint."

"It's strong in me."

"I'm sure it is, but I can't feel it."

Monroe acted interested. Lydia could not tell if he really was, or was merely avoiding her, or lost in his own thoughts again, as he usually was, and she was restless, and crossed her legs, and uncrossed her legs, and fiddled with the buttons on her blouse.

Later that night, they watched a movie. The movie was about a fire in a hotel where a man appeared to have taken his wife with the intention of killing her by pushing her out the window of their room on the fifteenth floor, but since there was a fire, they were trapped, together.

"I want to tell you about Martha," Lydia said.

"Do it, for goodness' sake."

She told him how Martha and Bob had lived together all these twenty some years, but had secretly divorced, legally, on paper, years ago, because Bob told her he wanted to sleep with other women, but would not, as long as he was legally married, so they divorced, but stayed on in the same house, for the children.

"And I said, Martha, are you crazy, or what? You went along with this, and I asked her, I said, did you keep making love, or what? Or was there nothing.

Nothing, at all, and she got defensive, and wouldn't talk about it."

————

MARTHA, NOT WATCHING the movie, was also trapped, but not by the flames of hell, or the flames of love, but by the weight of sodden anger, as if she'd swallowed bricks of peat and they'd gone to her legs, and so, still in this house with this man, not in a hotel where things could change, where she could jump, or shove him out, but on the first floor of a one-storied house, she cleared the dishes and began to wash them, and Bob stood in the doorway, watching her, and waiting for her to turn off the faucet. When she did, he moved in.

"See that faucet?" he asked.

"This one?"

"That one."

"Yes," she said.

"What did I tell you about that faucet?" he asked.

"What did you tell me?"

"Yes. What."

"Ummm, did you tell me something about it?"

"Right."

"How to do something about it, or with it, or what was it?"

"Dense," he said, and looked away. "Still dense, always will be, no memory, no learning capacity, no nothing."

"That's me, I guess," she said.

"It's just like my teaching you how to downshift when we first got together. I tried and tried to teach you how to use the clutch to gear down the speed of the car and save the brakes, but you couldn't get it."

"I tried. I did try."

"It's always something. You see, I'm the one who

has to replace the washers in that faucet assembly. Me."

"Well, you have my gratitude for that, you certainly do," she said, and batted her eyes at herself, at her reflection in the window over the sink.

"Tell me what I told you about turning it off."

"I can't remember. I truly cannot."

"You turn it off, gently."

"Oh right. Gently."

"I told you why, did I not?"

"I think so."

"And what did I tell you?"

"You said to turn it off. Gently."

"Why?"

"Why? Because, ummm, something about the washer?"

"Right. Because twisting it hard, like you do, like you want to wring it off," he said, and she nodded at herself in the window, "cuts the rubber washer as it contacts the base supply, and when it does that, it begins to drip, and when it drips, we waste water, and when it drips, I hear it, and when I hear it, I get mad."

"I'm sorry."

"Give me your hand," he said.

"Which one?"

"I don't give a damn which one."

He forced her hand over the faucet. Then, with both of his hands, over her one, he bent her fingers to fit the handle, as if she, herself, were doing it, voluntarily, and then he squeezed her fingers so hard, she felt the metal cutting into her bones, and he made her turn it off, again and again, the way he wanted.

"Now, do you understand?" he asked.

She did not answer.

"Do you have it imprinted now, in that slow-motion circuitry of yours?"

She looked out the dark window, and saw herself.

"Don't make me have to show you that again."

The mouse that lived below the sink, under the cabinets, and usually entered the kitchen this time each evening to get supper, had already skipped out the hole in the siding so he could get to the meeting on time.

THE PEOPLE IN the houses argued, and some of them attempted sleep, and some of them paced, and some of them found love, and some of them chased the youngsters around. It seemed like fun, and Ronnie hung from her window by her fingers, pretending her room was on fire, and Lydia teased Monroe about the show.

"He wasn't going to push her out," she said.

"Sure. Sure he was."

"People don't go that far."

"Some do. I see them all the time. And the ones who don't invent religions and so forth."

"Maybe."

"Or they end up like Martha."

"Maybe."

"Let's just watch the film and see what happens," he told her, but she left the couch, and threw away the tabloid she'd bought, which had an article she'd found humorous about the size of various anatomical parts of men and women, and after she threw that away, she reached under the mattress and removed the ruler, and put it back in the desk drawer.

FINALLY, MOST PEOPLE got to sleep, one way or another, but the air was still moist, and the air was still fraught, and static stung the lips of children who crept from their beds to peer out the windows, and the grown-ups hung from the ceiling, trying it out, to see if that would work, but the signals were charged in the air.

Sometimes, it felt like, to people considered and often diagnosed to be insane, that the signals were being received through their teeth, their fillings, or through their ears, which they then poked out with ice picks to stop the transmission.

If the airwaves were really as full as it was thought, and reception of everything broadcast was possible, even with the sets turned off, even with the radios in the off position, as was now thought to be true, then it was possible the man who had invented his own religion had honestly received a message from God, confused with other messages broadcast at that time, and it might have been he was doing what he'd been told to do, because, historically, there was a precedent for that religious role for women, and in some ways, it might have been kinder to induct one thousand members than to shove women out the fifteenth floor of a hotel, which one of the signals being broadcast was advocating that night, or breaking their bones over the metal handle of a kitchen faucet.

Outside, in the shadows, in the backyard of an empty house, the animals in the neighborhood met for the meeting. The dog that had seen Ronnie fall, was in charge, and after some confusion, barking, mewing, peeping, chirping, and the like, he got them quiet and began. There was a lot to talk about, and not much time.

RONNIE ARRANGED HER OLD cowboy and cowgirl ranch sets, and created different scenarios. Later, she looked out the window. She saw Monroe, the curious, handsome man next door, taking out the trash, and saw her mother ordering her father around the yard as he watered and nurtured the roses, and she thought about throwing a doll out the window, and knocking her mother in the head, and calling to her, just before she let it fly, so that it might sail through the air, a substitute for herself, and then, as her mother looked up to the voice calling her name, the doll would land in her face.

She did not act this out, because she wished she could find peace with the old woman and wished she could figure out what she'd done, however long ago it was, sometime after she'd forgotten to be the way she was expected to be, sometime after she'd forgotten to use the words she'd been taught to use, in the way she'd been taught to use them instead of making up her own words and putting them together in the way that felt good to her, in the way that felt wild, and made her laugh at the faces of everyone who stepped back, or leaned to one side, listening to her language.

So she did not throw the doll, but longed for peace, and contemplated how she'd gain it, and watched the handsome man next door, and then, before he could get back inside, she ran down the stairs and burst through the hedge and stopped face to face with him.

"Well," he said. "It's you. Again. I see you're all right."

"All right. Of course."

"I did not know you were pretending the other day."

She tried to hear how she should sound with this man, but nothing came clear right away.

He studied her face, her bones, her eyes, the shape of her eyes, her musculature, trying to find a sign that would tell what there was about her that seemed off. As he looked directly into her eyes, to study their clarity and how they focused and the contrast within, she suddenly fell forward into him, so that he either had to catch her in his arms, which he did, or let her hit the ground.

"You look like Roy," she said.

LYDIA MET MARTHA for an early lunch. The restaurant was in a cotton mill that had been converted to a shopping mall. There were exposed beams in the ceiling, and above them, the three-inch-thick flooring that had withstood so much hard work over its long life. There were chairs now, scattered tastefully about, that would have felt like heaven itself to have sat in, on any long, hot, twelve-hour day of work, in that cotton mill, one hundred years earlier.

"Well," Martha began, "I think I am finally, and I do mean finally, about to see the light."

"Well, good," Lydia said. "What light?"

Martha and Lydia were the same age, and had known each other since high school.

"It's taken me a long time, I know, but when you get messed up, it's hard to get straightened out again. But I think I am on my way."

"Great."

"What I figured out, was, that I needed a job. Now that the children are in college, I figured out, as if it were some kind of amazing revelation that I needed to get out, and be on my own."

"So you have a job? Is that it?"

"I do have one, at the, well . . . , at the prison, at the county prison unit, teaching the inmates how to cook."

"Really? In a prison?"

"I don't work inside the jail. It's in the kitchen, and in a classroom. I'm classified as an instructor, personnel-wise, that is."

"But in a prison? I mean, Martha, let's stop a minute and think. In a prison with murderers and rapists and all that? I mean, Martha, are you sure you're doing a good thing here?"

"It's not that kind of place. It's a county unit. A minimum security kind of place where people go for just small things, like not paying fines, or first offense drug possession, you know, like one marijuana cigarette, or something."

"Oh."

"And a lot of these men, I promise, haven't really done anything at all."

"Is that what they told you?"

"Yes. But I've asked other people and they've told

me the same thing. They're there, mostly, as a combination of bad luck, being too poor and too ignorant to hire good lawyers, and sometimes just plain revenge."

"By whom?" Lydia said, and moved her hands off the table so the waiter could set her plate in front of her.

"Their wives, ex-wives, girlfriends, cops who have it in for them, stuff like that."

"Oh."

"Bosses and people who wanted to get them back for this or that. A lot of them really shouldn't be there, at all."

IN THE BACKYARD, Monroe called to Ronnie as she disappeared through the break in the hedge.

"Wait. Don't run off."

She stopped. He could just see her through the branches and leaves and vines.

"Let's talk."

She waited.

"Who's Roy?"

She ran off then, without answering, and went in the back door, up the stairs, and into her room. She rummaged around in her closet until she found an old paint-by-numbers set that had been given to her years ago. She selected a western scene with cacti in the foreground, and mountains behind, and a few long-horn cattle between.

After that, she flipped through a stack of old Annie Oakley comic books she'd found in her closet, and paced around in her room as if she were locked in, walking against one wall, and bumping into it with her hands, and then shoving off of that wall and walking to the next, bumping into it, and then again back to the other one, and again.

I've got to do something, she thought. And soon.

WHILE WAITING FOR dessert, Lydia began to tell Martha something that happened the night before.

"So these two British guys were on this island, and they were filming the natives, real pretty-looking brown-skinned people with lovely hair and fine features, and the native men were wearing, well, what were they wearing? Not much, I guess is how you'd describe it, and the women were topless . . ." she was saying when Martha interrupted her.

"They never show white women topless. They always do if they're natives, though."

"But there was this one man, and he really looked good, and he was only wearing this loincloth-looking thing, but I think it was made out of leather, with just strings tied around his waist, and . . . ,"

"They never show naked men on television," Martha said.

"Well, these men were mighty close to it. But anyway, what I'm trying to get at is that I was watching this man, the leader of the tribe, the one with the leather loincloth, and I mentioned something about him, and . . . ,"

"What'd you say?"

"I don't remember. Something like, I wonder what it'd be like to be with someone like that, and you know what I meant by that, and so did Monroe, because he tossed this magazine he'd been reading up in the air and walked out of the room."

"Men," she said.

"I know. Men. But I swear, you know what it is? They want you to be sexual, but only with them. They want to be able to tell you when to be sexual, and then control it, so you aren't when they don't want you to be."

"I guess. I'm not sure," Martha said.

"I mean, you either are or you aren't. And I am."

"We all are, Lydia."

"I wish I could figure all this out. I really do. I do like Monroe. I surely do hope it works out this time. I'm tired of starting over again with a new man all the time."

"I'm not."

"I guess you wouldn't be."

"There's this guy at work, anyway."

"Oh?"

"He's so sweet. So big and rough and coarse on the outside, but sweet and tender and warm, inside. I'm really interested in him."

"What's he in for?"

"Nothing. He's one of those guys I was telling you about who didn't do anything. Not really. He got framed. He told me all about it."

MONROE WAS A PHYSICIAN in the emergency
room at the hospital. The emergency room, like most
others across the nation, had changed its name to the
trauma center, but it was the same. Monroe had never
wanted a private practice, and the work here, anony-
mous, urgent, and intense, suited him fine. He worked
three twelve-hour days one week, and then, four
twelve-hour days the next.

At nine one night, Monroe found time to take a
break, and he phoned Lydia. She was reading a magazine article about the history and evolution of making
love. After they talked a few minutes, Monroe had to
return to work, and Lydia continued reading, and then
fell asleep in the chair.

The phone rang again, and then later at eleven-
fifteen, and this time it was Monroe, who usually called
her just before she went to bed, when he was at work.

"Oh, hi," she said.

"Were you asleep?"

"For a second. In the chair."

"It's a slow night here. Mercifully."

"That's good."

"It won't last. Most of the trouble starts about now, about the time the alcohol and drugs have either had time to take full effect or wear off. Then, four or five in the morning, it slows down again."

"I wish you could come home."

"I do, too."

"I've been reading an article about when people started making love."

"I would have presumed that began about the time people began."

"But not like that. Like we do today."

"You mean it's different?"

"In one of the sections, on oral sex, they said, well, wait a minute. Is it all right to talk about this on the phone you're on?"

"Sure."

"Anyway, this guy who wrote the article, he was, or is, a sexual anthropologist," she said, and Monroe rolled his eyes toward the ceiling, "and he did this study of literature and stuff, and discovered that the first time anyone had ever done oral sex, or mentioned it, was in the twelfth century."

"Are you sure?"

"That's what he said. It started in Holland, or whatever they called that country back then, and that's where people invented it."

"Oh."

"And what's more, people didn't even kiss back then. Not like we do, nowadays."

"Some article," he said.

"And I was thinking, I sure am glad they got around to inventing it, kissing and all the rest, because the world surely would be missing out on something if they hadn't, but then I thought heck, if everything had to be invented, about lovemaking, then, what things have *not* been invented, and what are we missing out on now?"

"Not much, in your particular case," he said.

"But think about it. What else could there be?"

"I don't know."

"I wish I knew what it was going to be, the new stuff, I mean," she said.

"I agree. I wish I knew many things that were to be, as well. But that's life, and I'd like to talk all night about this, but I see they need me down the hall, so I've got to hang up."

"Okay. But one more thing. I forgot to tell you. Cissy called after you hung up last time, and they want us to go out with them on their new boat this weekend."

"Sure."

"Good. Well, then, I'll hang up, but I miss you, baby, and wish you could be here. I certainly do wish that."

"I do, too. But I'll see you in the morning."

NEXT DOOR, THE light was on in Ronnie's room, and she was awake, as were her mother and father in their separate rooms.

Mrs. Cutler peered through the keyhole of the mortised lock in Ronnie's bedroom door, and saw her on the floor, looking at a photograph in an old frame. The woman in the picture was Mr. Cutler's mother's grandmother. Ronnie's great-great-grandma.

Had things been different, between Mrs. Cutler and her daughter, she might have been softened by the sight of her child awake and alone at night, quietly reminiscing about her family, about their family. It should have touched her deeply, and it should have warmed her heart, and she should have tapped lightly on the door, and entered.

She should have sat across from Ronnie and told her everything she knew about the woman in the picture, and she and Ronnie could have talked the night away, and become intimate again, in the purest, most reliable sense of the word.

But she did not do that. Instead, she flung open the door, and grabbed the picture out of Ronnie's hands, and walked out.

"Get to bed," she yelled, and shoved the photo into a drawer in her own room, and went downstairs.

In the kitchen, Mrs. Cutler stared into the refrigerator a long time, as if she'd either forgotten what she wanted, or was just then deciding. She finally removed a pint of fresh blueberries. She put half of them into a bowl, and sprinkled sugar on top of them, and then covered them with cream.

She ate rapidly, distractedly, at the pace at which her heart was pounding, and then, just as suddenly as she'd begun, she stopped.

Alone, then, at the kitchen table, in the middle of the night, and eating blueberries with cream, brought something back to her, and made her uneasy. She did not know what to make of it, but she began to feel homesick, as if deep down she was being reminded of something.

The homesick longing was not for the house they'd left when they moved to this one, but for something further back, longer ago, and despite the fact that she gave in to her longing, she could not capture it.

She then resumed eating, but more slowly, and she finished what was left, and drank the remaining mixture of cream and sugar and juice.

Then, still lost in the feelings that had taken her

so by surprise, and, as if she'd lost track of not only what time of night it was, but of what time in her life it was, as well, she prepared another bowl of the same, and took it to her husband's room.

Her husband was lying in the bed, in the dark, with his eyes open. The light from the hall illuminated him like a corpse, pale and white as the sheets around him, with his hands clasped over his chest, and he did not move at all as his wife entered.

"Blueberries," she said.

LATER THAT NIGHT, in the emergency room, Monroe and a fellow doctor sat across from each other. A table was between them. On this table was a stack of magazines. Beside the stack, other magazines were scattered about, and with them, Styrofoam cups and candy wrappers. In the middle of that, Monroe and his colleague rested their feet.

"Did you see the woman with the knife wound in her back?" Monroe asked.

"Only for a moment. I saw her in passing."

"She was tall. She was six feet, or more. Maybe six two."

"Is that so?"

He was half asleep, and drinking coffee.

"She might have been more," Monroe said. "Prone like that, before she was covered up, she looked as if she went on and on. I thought, women are getting taller. They must be. It used to be rare when you saw a woman who was taller than a man, or, at least, as tall as a tall man."

"Right."

"But now, I see them all the time. I wonder about it. I don't think men are actually getting taller, but I have not read any research on it. Have you?"

"Not that I recall."

"But I would like to locate a study and see if I am right."

"You might be," the friend said.

"I don't know about men, but I am sure women are taller than they used to be and there are more women, for instance, from five feet nine to six feet, or six two, than ever."

"Black women, maybe."

"Well, yes, I was not thinking only of them, but both races, I believe."

"But not the Chinese. Not the Japanese," the other doctor said, not really caring one way or the other.

"Well no. I suppose I do mean Anglos or blacks. I suppose I do."

"You rarely ever see an oriental woman six feet tall."

"True," Monroe said.

"The only change I see in women is that they're happier now, than they used to be. Or so it seems to me," the other doctor said.

"Not the ones we see in here."

"No. I don't mean that. But in the general population. I would bet on that."

"Maybe."

"I think they are."

Monroe was silent for a minute, and then said, "I just had this vision of a world full of happy women, and it depressed the hell out of me."

"Why?" the other doctor asked.

"There's something depressing about a happy woman."

"Oh, I get it," the other doctor said, and laughed. "Taller, happier women, and where does that leave us?" he said, and laughed again.

Then they both laughed, and finished their coffee, and on the way down the hall the other doctor slapped Monroe on the back, and chuckled again.

LYDIA DID NOT WANT to get out of bed. She did not want to go to work.

"Phone in sick," Monroe suggested. He had just arrived and was beside her.

"No. I'm going. I need the money."

"You've got sick pay," he said.

"I might need it later."

"I make enough for both of us."

"That doesn't work either."

"I don't mind."

"It just doesn't work. It changes things."

Lydia was an admissions representative in the same hospital where Monroe worked. She helped people fill out the forms and become properly admitted.

"If you say so."

After she left, Monroe took the newspaper out of the blue plastic bag in which it had been delivered, and opened it up. He fell asleep in the same chair Lydia had fallen asleep in the night before.

Ronnie came out the back door, went through the break in the hedge, and quietly entered Monroe's house.

She was barefoot, wearing jeans and a white blouse. The blouse was tucked in, and the jeans were tight, and Ronnie's waist was small and she had combed her hair, and left it long, hanging down her back.

She saw Monroe asleep. She looked in the other rooms, and then sat opposite him. His mouth was open. His lips and his nostrils moved slightly in with each breath, and then out. There were three separate long gray hairs on the side of his head. The rest of his hair was brown, and stylishly long, but not too long. The way the three gray hairs looked, so out of place, made Ronnie want to pull them out.

He smelled funny. He smelled like a hospital. She leaned forward to discover what the card hanging from his shirt pocket meant. It was the same kind of card she'd seen in hospitals and schools on the people who worked there.

She contemplated the sleeping man. She wondered what he was like. She still wondered what she would have to do, and how she might have to act, to get him to like her. She pondered how she could be, and what she could be, and how far she could go, and just what he would like.

Monroe slept. Ronnie tiptoed to the bedroom and looked at Lydia's clothes. Then she removed her blouse, under which she wore nothing, and her jeans, under which, nothing as well, and pulled the top sheet back from the pillows and got in bed.

She covered herself with the sheet and sniffed the bed. She could smell Monroe and she could smell the woman, and she lay as if she were asleep, waiting.

He did not awaken. Soon she was restless. She put her clothes back on, and returned to the chair, and watched. He had changed positions. His head was still back, however, and his mouth was still open, and she crossed the room and stopped directly in front of him, and stuck her finger in his mouth.

She did this so carefully he never knew it happened. She aimed her finger between his lips and teeth and suspended it in the warm, wet air of his mouth, and then pulled it out again and put it to her nose, and then her tongue, as if trying to get an idea of how he tasted, the way you'd stick your finger in the batter of a homemade cake before you cooked it.

She looked down at his waist. She wondered if she could unzip his trousers without his knowing, and she tried it, but the moment she touched his zipper, he opened his eyes. She ran to the chair across the room and folded her legs beneath her, so that she was on her knees, and she covered her mouth with both her hands, so he could not see she was laughing. He stared at her, startled and uncomprehending.

"What are you doing?" he asked.

"Well, doing nothing," she replied.

"How long have you been here?"

"Not long."

She listened to her voice, and began to hear something new in it that she liked, and she followed it.

"I saw her leave," she said.

"Who?"

"The woman."

"You mean Lydia?"

"Your woman."

"I guess you do mean Lydia. You haven't met."

"No."

"And frankly, you and I have not met. Not really. Not formally."

"But I know you."

"My name is Monroe."

"Monroe," she repeated.

"M-o-n-r-o-e," he said, and spelled it.

"M-o-n-o-r-o-e," she misspelled it back.

"No," he said, and then let it go. "But that's close enough. It's just Monroe. It's an old family name, as you might surmise."

She nodded.

"But what's your name?"

"Ronnie," she said. "R-o-n-o-r-o-e."

He smiled, and she did too.

"I suppose I did not have to spell it, did I?"

She shook her head.

"I've wondered about you ever since I saw you in the yard last week. What were you doing?"

"Falling."

"I know, but why?"

"Just falling."

"Do you fall often?"

"Yes."

"Do you like to fall?"

"Yes."

"Do you get hurt?"

"No."

"And how long have you been falling?"

"Forever."

"I see."

"Like this," she said, and rose, and then fell backward into the chair. She fell slowly, though, or so it seemed to Monroe, as if she had perfected, or actually learned, how to fall in slow motion, to defy gravity, and she settled into the chair with her hands at her sides and then closed her eyes, but only for a few seconds before she laughed out loud.

"Like that," she said, and chuckled some more.

"But what does it mean?"

"It means," she said, and floated her hand and arm into the air, and around in a circle, and then lowered it gracefully like the gesture of a ballet dancer, "it means, like that," she said, and did it again.

"I don't understand."

"It's fine. You do not have to."

He paused as he struggled for something to say, something to do, to keep her there, to give him more time to understand what she was about.

"Have you had breakfast?"

"Yes and no," she said.

"Does that mean you'd like more?"

"Yes."

"Let's make some, then," he said, and she followed him into the kitchen.

"What does that mean?" she asked, pointing to his tag.

"That's my identity card."

"But what does it mean?"

"It means I have permission to be in the hospital, doing certain permissible things."

"It tells you that?"

"It tells who I am to other people."

"And to yourself?" she asked.

"In a way, yes."

"Then I must have one," she said.

"I could get you something like this, I suppose, if you really want one."

"How does a girl get one, exactly like that?"

"You'd have to be a doctor, and be employed where I am employed."

"I could do that."

"Yes, it's likely you could, but it might take some years to do it."

He took out the eggs and showed them to her,

and she shook her head no, and then he took some bacon from the refrigerator, and she indicated no to that as well, and then he pointed to a box of cereal, and she nodded yes, and they sat across from each other in the dining room and ate.

"Is this what you had for your first breakfast?"

"No. I had ... uh ... well," she said, and then stopped, and thought about it, and wondered how to tell him what it was, what it tasted like, and how to tell him all of this in the new way of speaking she had begun to invent and tailor for him, this time for him, and so she put her fork down, and was silent, and then said, "I had my mother."

"Your mother?"

"Your mother?" she repeated.

"What do you mean?"

"It tasted like my mother. I couldn't eat it."

"I see."

"I see," she said.

"Why did you repeat that?"

"Because I don't like the sound of it. Because it's what certain people always say to me when they ask me something and I answer them. Truthfully, I mean. The more you tell the truth to someone, the more they say, I see, and look at you funny."

Monroe tried not to look at her funny, and he tried so hard to be neutral in how he was looking at her, that she suddenly pushed her face forward, toward him, and bugged her eyes at him.

"Sorry," he said. "I was just thinking."

"I know you were."

"How old are you, Ronnie?"

"Seventeen. I mean, eighteen."

"Which is it?"

"Eighteen."

"Have you finished school?"

"Which school?"

"High school."

"Oh. Well, the last high school I went to was really a low school, and I never did feel high enough to finish it," she said, and then picked a raisin out of her cereal and tossed it at Monroe.

Monroe ignored the raisin, which hit his pants just below his belt, and asked, "So you haven't graduated yet?"

She didn't answer. She finished her cereal, and while she did, Monroe watched her, but said nothing more. He stared across the table at her, quietly and thoughtfully.

She looked up once, and saw him watching her, and she ran her finger around and around the rim of her bowl, and carefully blew into the milk that remained in the bottom of it, making it ripple gently, like the surface of a pond from a breeze.

"I guess you want to know about me," she finally said. "I don't mind that you do. I want you to know. I wasn't sure at first if I did want you to know all of it, but I think I do."

She left the bowl, with the spoon in it, on the table, and walked into the kitchen, and looked out the window at her own house, and then sat on the floor, leaning against the refrigerator, with her legs crossed Indian-fashion, as if settling in for a long powwow.

"Come on in here," she said.

Monroe stood across the narrow room, and crossed his arms, and tried to look pleasant, unconcerned, and relaxed.

"You don't have to tell me anything, Ronnie. Not anything at all."

"But I want to. I really do. Because, see, I really and truly have had a strange life, and I think you'd understand better than anyone, and I also think you do want me to tell you, because I think you want to know about me, because I think you like me. And because I like you, I want to go ahead and tell you everything.

"See, I had a kind of bad childhood. I was born out West, and we didn't have much money when I was growing up, and then something happened and I don't know what, but my parents got involved with that cult, that Jim Jones cult, and we all went down to Guyana, and my parents got killed down there, in that mass suicide thing," she said, and looked up for the first time since she began telling Monroe this story of her life, and saw him looking down at her and shaking his head in sympathy.

"Anyway," she went on, "that's one of the reasons I hate Kool-Aid, but they died down there, and then I don't remember very well what happened next, but I didn't die, and then I was flown up here, you might have read about it in the papers, I was in the papers when it happened, that's how I know so much about it, from reading all the news articles that were saved for me, but I was in the paper, this picture of me was all over, everywhere, everybody saw it, that little girl in someone's arms running to an airplane was me. Do you remember that?"

"Possibly," he said.

"And then I ended up here with my father's aunt and uncle. See, they're not my real parents. I bet you thought they were. But they're not. My real parents died down there in that Guyana thing, and I got stuck here with that monster for a mother and poor old Aloysius Cutler for a father, and then, I guess, things kind of went from bad to worse, and I've been getting into lots of trouble ever since.

"I come from good stock though. Tough stock. My ancestors were pioneers on the great plains, and I know all about them, and I'm part Indian, like a lot of people from out there, just a little part, but they were tough people, and lived hard, and my great-great-great-grandma, one time, when they were starving, out on the wagon train, had to try to feed everyone by making soup from hides and fur rugs, and then they had to eat the horses and finally, just before they were all about to die, she had to cook the dog, old Rascal, which is why I think that old woman next door is so mean, because she's part dog, don't you think she even looks like one, but then again, I was lucky, since I'm blood kin to all those people, the way it affected me, is that I can run so fast."

After she said that, she got off the floor, and returned to the table, passing Monroe without looking at him, and drank the leftover milk from her bowl.

"That made me dry, talking all that much," she said.

"I don't know what to say," Monroe told her. "I just don't know what to say."

"You don't have to say anything, but I bet you never, ever, never in your life met anyone like me before."

"No. I don't think I have."

"You look kind of pale, pardner. Don't take it so hard. I'm okay. I always will be, if'n I can figure out a way to git away from them crazy people over yonder who've been a-raising me all this time," she said, slipping into her cowgirl dialect.

"If I'm pale, and I apologize if I looked that way, it's not from your story, though that in itself could make a person feel faint, but it's from the fact that I have had no sleep for about twenty-four hours, and I am worn out. But your story, Ronnie, is extraordinary. Literally. Truly, it is."

"Shucks. I can survive anything. At least, I've learned that. I reckon I could eat a dog if'n I had to, but I shore would hate to eat one that was a pet."

"The will to live is strong."

"You betcher boots it is. That's why I'm a-gonna figure out a way to get away from them varmints next door what is driving me crazy."

"You'll soon be old enough," he said.

"I'm old enough now."

"Well, listen, Ronnie. I don't want to be rude, but I truly must get some sleep, and I want to thank you for coming over, and maybe we'll see more of each other, as time goes by."

"As time goes by," she said.

"I'm certain we will," he said, and walked toward the door, expecting her to follow. "Come by sometime and meet Lydia. You'll like her."

"Maybe."

"Either way, I need to take a shower and get some sleep."

"You go right ahead and take your shower," she said, "but I don't want to go home just yet. I'm feeling too good right now, and the minute I walk in that door I'll start feeling bad, so I'd like to hang around here a while longer, if it's okay."

"It might not be the right thing."

"As a matter of fact," she said, ignoring his answer, "I could do with a shower myself."

"That's certainly your business, all right, if you want to have a shower or not, but you run on home now while I have mine."

"I could take one here better."

"But it would be rather unusual, Ronnie, when you have a perfectly good means of doing that in your own home."

"The water there is bad."

"It's the same water."

"No. It is not."

"You have a well?"

"I do not know about a well, but the water there is bad."

"Why? Why is it bad?"

"It's yellow," she said.

"Yellow?"

"Or sometimes red. Not red, red, but yellowish-red."

"Oh. I see. Your pipes must be bad."

"It is not the pipes," she said. "It is something else."

"All right, then. I understand now. But it won't do, it just won't do to take your shower or bath here. Maybe later. Maybe after Lydia comes home. Talk to her about it."

"Will she like that?"

"Like what?"

"For me to take a shower with her?"

"No, Ronnie. I didn't mean that. Did you really think I meant that, or are you playing around with me?"

"Both," she said softly, and looked down.

"What I meant was that it would be better if you talked to Lydia about it."

"I don't want to."

"Well, what is it you want?"

"I would like to take a shower with you. First with you, and then, if you wanted me to, and if it would make you happy, then with Lydia. I would do that, if you wanted me to do it."

"Oh my," he said.

He said oh my, like that, because if you attached him to a lie detector and asked him if he wanted to take a shower with this lovely, strange girl, and he had the gall to answer, no, the fuses would have blown from the enormity of the lie. Of course he wanted to.

"It's not possible. At some different time, somewhere, but not now. Not here. Not with me. With someone else, yes, Ronnie, you are correct, it would be nice. But not with me."

"Then you don't want me to?"

"It's not wanting you to, or not wanting you to. It's what should be, and shouldn't be."

"Then I will wait for you. I will wait here," she said, and pointed to the chair.

She was there when he returned. His hair was wet. He wore baggy work pants and a work shirt that matched. On the shirt was a label, and within the label was sewn the name, Lloyd.

"A new name," she said.

"Oh. That's just there. Lydia bought these for me at a yard sale. I wear them around the house."

"I will call you Lloyd."

"No. Don't do that."

He picked up a ceramic figurine that had fallen over on the table beside the chair where Ronnie sat. It was a small model of a Victorian lady with a parasol and a surprised, but coy, expression on her face.

"Did you make that?" Ronnie asked.

"No. I bought it at the same yard sale Lydia bought these clothes," he said. "I don't even know why I bought it."

"It looks like Lydia, a little," she said.

"No. It does look, in some bizarre, exaggerated way, like someone else I used to know."

"She's kind of cute," Ronnie said, holding it in her hand and looking at it from all sides.

"I don't want to be rude, Ronnie, but truly, I am exhausted, and I need some sleep. I've been at work all night, and it's not doing me any good to alter the pattern of sleep I've adjusted to."

"All right."

"Come back again, and meet Lydia. I'm certain she'll be interested in you."

"I doubt it," Ronnie said.

"She will."

"You smell nice, by the way."

"That's the soap. It's something Lydia splurges on. She likes it."

"I do, too."

"Here, then," he said, and walked quickly to the bathroom and brought her an unopened bar, "take this, and enjoy it."

Ronnie left, and Monroe went to his room and went to sleep. Ronnie paced around her room, and looked at herself in the mirror, and bonked herself in the head a few times with a knocked silly, knocked cuckoo look on her face, and then she ran past her mother, who was asleep in front of the television, and out the door, and down the street.

ON THE WEEKEND, LYDIA and Monroe went to the lake as planned. On the way there, they argued.

"The skirt is all right," he said, "and by that I mean that kind of skirt on some people is fine, and then again, on others, it simply, quite simply, Lydia, does not work."

"What kind of people is it all right on?"

"Just different kinds. It's not you. I don't care, really, if you're wearing it. But you asked my opinion, and I told you."

"You mean it looks better on younger women. Is that what you mean?"

"Partly."

"On girls. Is that it?"

"Not entirely."

"I may have just slipped over into that forty-something group, but I can tell you this, big boy. My legs are just as good as any little college girl's you could find anywhere."

"True. That's true. You do have good legs."

"Then what is it?"

"It's nothing. Let's forget it."

"Do you know something, Monroe?"

"Tell me."

"I do not believe that anyone, not anyone in my life since I left home, has tried to tell me what kind of clothes to wear."

"I'm not trying to do that."

"I do not believe that anyone since my father has ever tried to tell me that I was wearing a skirt that was too short."

"I didn't say that."

"I'll wear any damn thing I want. Or nothing at all, if I want to do that. Nothing, you hear?"

"Fine. Go right ahead. You have my permission to go to town naked from now on."

"I don't need your permission."

"True. That's true."

"This is so strange. I think you're jealous of Roger. You know he has the hots for me, and always has."

"I do know that, but it does not concern me. It's his problem."

"Oh, how cute."

"You may have subconsciously chosen that skirt to give him a thrill, or you may not. Neither you, nor I, will ever know."

"Look. I mean, Roger, you know. Well, he's just a man. He's just another man."

"I see," he said, but with a puzzled look on his face.

"Forget it."

"I don't think I will. Maybe you two need some time alone. I'll see if I can arrange it."

"You creep," she said.

"Look," he said and nodded toward the parking lot. "Here they come."

"I've got my bathing suit on under this thing anyway."

"Good," he said. "One would hope you had something under it."

"You don't know when to stop," she said, and then waved to Roger and Cissy.

"I'll stop when you stop," he said.

"I could wear a skirt up to my waist and it wouldn't matter. It's my bathing suit under it."

"I'm glad."

"Jesus, you are making me so mad. I haven't been this mad, I don't think, ever, with you."

"Oh, sure you have," he told her, and patted her on her shoulder and walked on ahead to meet their friends.

"I don't like this at all," she said, and caught up with him and held his arm. "I had a whole childhood of people telling me what to do, and what to think, and a couple of husbands as well. I thought I was through with it."

"You are."

"Damn," she said, but mostly to herself, "if you want me and Roger together, then you got it, big boy."

She ran toward the couple. She gave Cissy a big hug and kissed her on her cheek and then jumped onto Roger, and kissed him on the lips, and wrapped her legs behind his, completely off the ground, and fully against him.

On the boat, Lydia started drinking right away, and she and Roger began to match each other, beer for beer. Then, in the middle of the lake, and on their way to the cove in which they would anchor for lunch, Cissy went below to prepare the food, and Monroe went with her. Lydia left Roger steering the boat, and went forward, climbed over the roof of the cabin, jumped past the windshield, and landed on the deck as far forward as she could get. She took off her skirt and her blouse, under which she wore her two-piece.

"Looking good," Roger called.

She saluted him, and then did a military about-face, and marched, with a bit more undulation than the military would have allowed, up to a mast, and propped her feet against the sides of the boat where the sides folded above and over the deck, and leaned back, facing the sun, with her hair down her back and her eyes closed and her arms behind her, as if she were tied to the post.

"You look like the figure on the front of an old sailing vessel," Roger called, and Lydia leaned forward, the better to imitate the pose.

Then she settled back against the post and closed her eyes, and began to relax. The way she began to relax surprised her, because until she leaned back, and felt the sun deep within, she had not realized how tense she'd been. Once she realized it, she let herself go, and began to feel good again, and sleepy, and warm. Roger called to her, but she did not respond. She quite suddenly, and quite thoroughly, wanted nothing more to do with him the rest of the day, and was also annoyed at herself for having led him on the way she had.

"A salad's really the only thing that works on an outing such as this," Cissy told Monroe, who was carving slices of country ham and then chopping them into smaller pieces while they talked.

"It certainly would not be worth cooking a hot meal," he said.

"Not on a summer afternoon, anyway," she said. "At night, on a cool night, it's all right. But not today."

They were making small talk, each trying not to think about the foolishness of their partners, above. It was not even enough to be jealous over. It was embarrassing, if anything.

"The salt in that ham will give a balance to this salad," she said. "Sometimes a little herring or smoked salmon is great, also."

"But probably not along with the ham," he said.

Roger throttled back the engine, and Lydia opened her eyes and saw they were turning into the cove, and closed her eyes again. The cove was deep and long and they were alone in it, and Roger let the boat idle toward its mooring, while he sneaked along the side of the cabin toward Lydia.

"We're almost there," Cissy said. "Dump in what you have chopped up, and put the rest away."

"I can finish. Just a few more seconds," Monroe said, and peered out the window in time to see Roger crawling along the deck.

"Who knows why?" Cissy said, and shrugged, as she saw him, as well. "He turns into a high school kid out here."

Silently Roger rose up behind Lydia and kissed her on her neck.

"Gotcha girl," he said and reared back dramatically as if to ward off a punch.

Lydia fell forward, away from him, and when she did the strap from her top caught on a tie-down hook, which was fastened to the post, and she lost her top.

"Sorry about that, old girl," he said, and, after getting a good look, averted his eyes and retrieved the bathing suit top and handed it to her.

"Damn," she said, and covered herself with it, and looked at it. "The snap is ripped out."

"I've some safety pins down here," Cissy offered.

She and Monroe had rushed up when they heard the scuffling.

"What was that all about?" Monroe asked a few minutes later, sitting on a bench behind Roger, who was steering the boat around the perimeter of the cove, looking for a good, sandy spot where they could eat.

"She snagged her suit on one of those tie downs," he said. "Damn awkward thing to happen."

The outing ended early. Lydia and Monroe drove off, waving goodbye to Cissy and Roger, who were going to spend the night on the boat at the marina.

Monroe had handed Lydia the keys, so she was driving.

"I suppose I'm driving so you can pout all the way home."

"Pouting's not good for you," he said. "It's a form of stress. Cardiovascular and all that."

"Oh thank you for the illumination."

"Pouting is anger, you know. Stifled anger. I'm not angry, so therefore, ergo, and all that, I couldn't be pouting. I might be curious, but not angry. Definitely not angry."

She explained what had occurred, and how.

"I suppose you believe I hooked myself onto that tie down on purpose, so I could give Roger a show."

"It's possible."

"Well, I did not."

"Not consciously, one would presume."

"Not any way."

"Good."

"God, I hate it when you get like this. We've been at each other since we got up this morning. Can't we just stop? I didn't mean to do that. You know I didn't."

"Of course not."

"You say that, but you don't mean it. What are you upset about? What? I can't imagine. I have no idea. None. None at all."

"Nothing," he said, and leaned against the window and closed his eyes.

"I guess it's up to me," she said, and sighed. "Okay. It's my fault. I did it all. I made a mess of everything. I know I came on a bit too much, you know, with Roger, but then, when I got up to the front of the boat, I suddenly came back to myself, my true self, you know, from wherever else I'd been, and suddenly there with my true self back within me, I felt this kiss on my neck, and I knew, I just knew it wasn't you, not that you wouldn't kiss me, but I knew it was him, that bozo, and I just leaped away, and that's when it happened.

"I don't even like him, Monroe. I don't. I can't even stand him, not really. It's just that, I got into that thing I do sometimes, where, when something goes wrong, instead of being calm about it, I go the opposite way, and make it worse.

"I've always done that. I don't know where it comes from. Maybe from watching my mother, who just lay down like a doormat and let my father walk all over her, but I've told you all that already, but the point is, the thing is, when I get like that, I can't stop myself, and so, it's not me, really, not my true self, doing it. It's not."

"Your true self?" he asked, a bit sarcastically.

"Well, laugh if you want, but I mean it. And besides, you're not entirely blameless in all of this. But that's not the point. It's over. I went too far. I flirted with that creep, and he bought into it, and it was a mistake."

"Good."

"I was doing it, anyway, to make you see how foolish you were acting."

"Oh. Well, then, let's forget it, and move on."

"But then, I got going and couldn't stop. It's like I have this thing where, I can't stand things to go wrong, and when they do, I make them go more wrong."

"You said that already."

"See, what I should have done is not pay any attention to you this morning, and then I wouldn't have gotten my dander up, and then I wouldn't have flirted with Roger, which made you more distant, and madder . . ."

"I wasn't mad."

"And then I wouldn't have gotten crazier because you were thinking I was crazy, and then I wouldn't have gone up there and got hooked on that thing . . ."

"Let's not go over every detail a hundred times, all right. Just drive. It happened. It's over. I don't care."

"I mean, do you think, I mean, you're a doctor, that really, in some subconscious way, I would have hooked myself onto that bracket and done that on purpose? Is that possible? Could I really have did that? I mean, done that to myself on purpose? Because if it is, then my goodness, what's next? I mean, how does anyone know if they're doing something because they really want to or because of something else? How?"

"Let it go, Lydia. It's just life. It's nothing to do with conscious or unconscious that anyone will ever know. It's just life."

"There's no way, really, that I could have maneuvered myself onto that hook and pulled my top off on purpose. Not subconscious purpose or anything else. There's no way."

"Stop."

"Okay. I'll stop. But I want to tell you something else about the skirt. I don't like it, either. I bought it, and then when I brought it home, I didn't like it myself. So why did I wear it? Because I bought it, I guess, and then I had to wear it, but I don't have to anymore, now that I know it's not right for me, so you know what?"

"What?"

"I'm going to throw it out the window," she said, and reached into the back seat for it.

"Don't do that. There's no need to waste it."

"Well, what then? How about, . . . let's see, . . . I know. How about this? We'll drive until we see a real poor person's house, and stuff it in their mailbox. Wouldn't that be neat? They'd open it up, and gosh, they'd think, where did that come from. Wouldn't that be fun?"

"It's against the law."

"Oh, it is not. It's no such thing. We could find somebody's house, the kind set way back off the road, like that one there," she said, and pointed to it as they sped by, "with no grass in the yard and cars and trucks pulled up everywhere, and stop there."

"Oh me," he sighed.

"You know, sometimes when you pass a house like that, you see someone on the porch. Sometimes it's this teenage girl, sitting on the steps with her knees up and her chin resting in her hands, and you think, as you whiz by in your fine car, that she's out there because she can't be in the house anymore with everyone else, and that she's outgrown the family, or she's changed, but they haven't, and maybe she's the oldest child, but then, also, she can't go anywhere because there's no money to go anywhere, and none of the

cars work, and she doesn't have any clothes to wear
that she likes."

"Cinderella," he said.

"No. Not like that. But haven't you seen someone
like that before, sitting on the steps, all by herself? I
have. I can remember so clearly seeing the face of
this real poor, but nice-looking girl with straight hair,
sitting out there, and I knew she was dreaming about
things, just sitting there, unable to go anywhere, and
dreaming. And we could stop at a house like that
and put the skirt in the mailbox, and something else
with it, a gift, maybe some money in the pocket, and
then drive off before they saw us. Wouldn't that be
great?"

"You know," he said, "if you put the skirt in the
mailbox, and money in the pocket, the first thing that
would occur is there'd be a fight over the skirt, and
someone would get shot over the money, or knifed,
or beaten up, and they'd end up in the emergency
room, with the skirt covered with blood, and ripped
up, and that would be the reality of your plan."

"Well, my God, Monroe. If that isn't just the
ugliest thing you've ever said since I've known you. I
swear. It really is."

"Okay. Go ahead and do it. I'm going to take a
nap."

"Well, kiss me before you do, then, so I'll know
it's over."

He turned away. He rested his head against the
towel bunched against the window like a pillow, and
tried to sleep. Lydia decided not to push any further,
and to disregard the absence of the kiss, and to let it
be over. She drove on. The car was nearly alone on
the old two-lane road. Along the road were small
houses. They were similar to the ones Lydia had

described. Every now and again, a larger, grander house appeared.

Ahead, a dog came out of the woods. The dog had its nose to the ground. It was following a trail. Another dog followed it. The lead dog ran the trail out of the woods and into the road. It never looked up.

Lydia saw the dog from the corner of her eye. It appeared the dog would do the sensible thing, and wait for her to pass. When it did not, she slammed on the brakes. At the same time, the second dog, still at the edge of the woods, must have signaled to the lead dog, who did stop, and the car slid past him.

After the car went by, the two dogs looked around in momentary confusion, as if they'd awakened in a strange place. They cleaned the saliva off their dripping jaws, swallowed, and continued on.

Monroe, himself awakening from his nap, did not swallow. Lydia did not either. Their mouths were dry.

"Did you hit it?" he asked.

"No."

"Good."

"I saw its face just as I missed it. It had a lovely face. With beautiful eyes."

"Yes," he said. "I remember moments like that."

"You do?" she asked, amazed he was talking to her again in a friendly way. "Like what?"

"I remember a woman brought in one time. She'd been hit, and then dragged under a car. Her skin was gone, mostly gone, where she had been dragged, and what was left was mixed in with her clothes, what was left of them. She was injured badly. She had nearly ceased to look human. I recall thinking, she looked something like the human body looked inside when I first observed a major surgical procedure—like raw meat."

"Oh, gosh," Lydia said.

"She looked like an animal with its fur gone. And yet, when I looked in her face and found her eyes, it was all there. I saw it all. Normally, you would expect a traumatized person's eyes to mirror the trauma within, but hers did not. I could see her soul, or whatever one would call that which made her what she was, still there, still alive, still unharmed. It was an unusual moment. A remarkable moment."

"Did she live?"

"Yes."

"But what was she like after you fixed her up?"

"All right. She was all right. Reconstructive technologies are so good these days, she made it back all right."

"Made it back all right," Lydia repeated.

"Correct."

"That's a strange way to put it."

"I suppose she's fine now. Physically, anyway."

"You saved her."

"No, I did not do that. I don't know what it is that saves a person. It isn't me. I know that."

"It was," she said. "I think it was."

She laid her hand on the seat between them. Her hand was open. The way it was open was unmistakably the way people laid their hands when they wanted them to be held by another person.

Lydia felt tender and open herself at that moment, and felt that he was the person she knew he was, knew he'd been, knew he'd always be, the person she knew she wanted to be with, the man she'd left her husband for, and she wanted Monroe to know how she felt about him.

"You're wonderful," she said. "You are."

The hand, however, remained by itself. He saw it.

He did not reach for it. Because he did not reach for it, it became a disembodied hand. It was merely a wrist, a hand, and some fingers. Lydia glanced at this hand, and it did not appear to be her own hand. It was, but it did not feel like it.

Maybe it had come off. Maybe her hand had come off, and that's why she couldn't feel it. Maybe that was it. It must have been. It must have been his rejection that severed her hand as easily as he could have done with his array of surgical instruments.

There should have been blood everywhere. He had sliced off her hand, and there it lay between them. She had offered her hand. She had not seen the knife.

THAT NIGHT, FEELING better, or trying to, Lydia phoned Martha. Martha wasn't home. Bob said he did not know where she was. Then Lydia phoned her mother.

Lydia's mother lived in a retirement community. She had sold her small house and given the money to the community in exchange for meals and care and a small apartment for the remainder of her life. Her mother enjoyed her life in this community, which was a three-hour drive from where Lydia and Monroe lived, and had many friends, and went out in the van as often as she could find something to do, or someone to accompany her.

"What a day," Lydia said. "First off, the boat. Well, how can I describe it to you. It was, well, spectacular."

"That's nice," her mother said.

"And the people what own it, I don't know how they've had the time to fix it up, what with him being a famous doctor and all, and being so busy, and she has all her society and charitable work to do, but they spend time together on that thing, and they've just restored it beautifully."

"I'm glad you had fun. Did Monroe enjoy himself?"

"Oh yes. So much. We laid around and got some sun, and he was so relaxed, he slept practically all the way home."

"I'd like to go on a boat," she said.

"Well, you have to have good legs," Lydia said. "I mean, strong legs, and good balance."

"Not that kind, dear," her mother said. "I mean, a cruise ship, like on television."

"Oh."

"That'd be nice, before I die."

"You're not going to die, Mother."

"I most certainly am. Not soon, I hope, but I will."

"You won't. Don't worry. Monroe could give you a checkup if you feel like something's wrong. Do you want me to talk to him about it?"

"No. I do not. And I do not need a checkup," she said, and then whispered, "especially by him," which she could not resist saying, though she tried to say it too softly for Lydia to hear.

"What?"

"Nothing."

"I heard that. I don't know when you're going to realize what a good doctor he is, and what a good person, too. I've finally found the right man, Mama. I finally did. After all those wasted years, and then ending up with that stupid Marcus who wouldn't let me have children, and now it's too late, I've finally found the right one."

"Uh huh," her mother said.

"Well, I have. You don't like him because you just

don't know him. You would if you ever got to know him."

"Uh huh."

"I don't understand how you could form such a stubborn opinion after only meeting him twice. I just don't understand it."

"There's something about him," she said.

"Like what?"

"I don't know. Something."

"Well, you're wrong."

"I doubt it. I might as well get ready to see you come running back to me one more time before you learn."

"Don't worry, Mama. I'm not going to have any trouble. I've figured out how to hold on to them by now, and he's different anyway. He's a doctor, Mama. He's educated. He's not like the rest of them."

"Uh huh."

"Anyway, who are you to talk? You didn't do so well yourself, now, did you?"

"No. That's how I know what I know."

"Okay. Okay. We won't start all that again. I'm sorry. I am. Anyway," she said, and took a deep breath, "I just wanted to tell you why I hadn't called earlier, and what a fab-u-lo-so time we had out there, and to let you know I'm thinking of you, and will be out to see you the first chance I get."

6

SUNDAY, MONDAY, AND TUESDAY, Monroe worked. He was then off four days, and on Wednesday he was reading when Ronnie came over.

"You've returned," he said.

"Yes."

"I saw you once. Going somewhere with your mom and dad."

"Yes. I did do that."

"What else have you been doing?"

"Watching you."

"Oh, have you, now?"

"Yes."

"You don't beat around the bush, do you?"

"No."

"That might not be the right way to be."

"I am just what I am. I am just the way I am. I cannot help it."

"And you've always been this way, whatever it is, the way you are?"

"Yes."

"Tell me about it."

"No."

While she talked, she paced around in front of him, then climbed on a chair and sat on the back of it, with her bare feet on the cushion.

"So now what?" he asked.

"You make me nervous," she said.

"I'm sorry. I don't mean to. You talk, then. I'll listen. Will that be better?"

"Maybe."

She said nothing after that, and finally Monroe spoke.

"Who's Roy, by the way?"

"I don't want to tell you. But you look like him. To me you do. You've got a good face, and strong arms. You look tough, but good. Like Roy."

"Is he an old boyfriend?"

"No."

"Okay. What else, then? What else do we want to talk about?"

"I hate my mother," she said. "I mean, that woman over there."

"I think I guessed that, but I don't know from what. Was it something you told me before?"

"I just hate her. I just want to get away from her. I used to want to, when I was little, run away and live with Roy and," she started to say something else, but then stopped, and wouldn't finish the sentence.

"Why do you hate her?"

She did not answer that either, but got off the chair and walked back and forth in front of Monroe, looking at him as she walked by, and biting on a fingernail, and thinking.

"I don't have much time," she finally said.

"For what?"

"For everything. I need to get rolling."

"I have that feeling sometimes," he said.

"I like your face."

"Thank you. I like yours, too."

"I know you do."

"Oh?"

"I can tell by the way you look at me."

"I see."

"Will you kiss me?" she asked.

It came out of nowhere so fast Monroe had no answer. He couldn't have been more caught off guard than if Lydia had walked in the room and caught him actually doing it. He felt that guilty about it already.

"Kiss you? Well, dear child, I don't know how to answer that."

"It is usually with a yes or a no."

"Well, it's not exactly a yes or a no. It could be, for instance, a maybe. Or something else, like not now."

"I wish it would be a yes."

"Ronnie, do you always talk to people this way?"

"No."

"To some people? To a few people?"

"Yes."

"Then I don't understand."

"I want you to kiss me. I have thought about it, and I want you to."

"But why?"

"Because I like you, and you make me feel strange, and it's time. It's time to be kissed."

"But I can't. It's like what you asked previously. About the shower. It would be wrong."

"It does not seem wrong to me."

"It would."

"It seems it would be wrong not to."

"No."

"Because I know you want to kiss me."

"You do not know that, Ronnie."

"I do."

"How do you know that, Ronnie?"

"Because, Monroe, you looked at my lips, and I could feel that's what you wanted to do."

"I did not."

"And since I could feel it, I thought you, too, could feel it from me."

"No, Ronnie. This is simply not going to happen. It simply is not."

"I will wait," she said.

"You are a mystery," he said, walking out onto the porch, with her following.

"I am not a mystery. I am just what I am. You are the mystery."

"Why is that?"

"You and everyone else. You want to say something, but you cannot. You want to do something, but you cannot. That is the mystery."

"You may be right."

"I am."

"Well, I must ask you, Ronnie. Is this the way it's going to be every time you come over?"

"Maybe."

"Talking like this, saying anything that pops in your mind."

"I only say what I think."

"That's what I mean."

"But I thought about it, long before I said it."

"I see."

"I still want to kiss you."

"Saying what you think," he told her, ignoring the last remark, "is often not the right thing to do."

"You know that is not true."

"I know it *is* true."

"You are saying that because you don't know what else to say."

"Never mind, then," he said.

He went back inside, and she followed him.

"You're smiling," he said.

"Yes. I just thought of something. But I won't say it. Not yet."

"I just realized you don't smile much."

"Nor do you."

"Is that right?"

"Yes."

"I've never been told that about myself."

"It's so. You have yet to do it today, so far."

He went to the couch and straightened the cushions.

"What would you like to do, then, and don't say what you've just been saying."

"I would like to sit beside you."

"And then what?" he asked, after she did.

"Read to me."

"What do you want me to read?"

"That book."

"Do you know what it's about?"

"No. I just want you to read to me. I just want to listen. I just want to feel the words and your voice. I don't care what it's about."

"Ronnie, I will have to say this. If I say it again and again, it will be true each time. I have never, ever, met anyone quite like you."

"Good," she said.

He read to her. Unexpectedly, it worked on him as well, and the more he read, the closer he felt, and the more he felt it, the more she felt it. It was one of the nicest moments he'd had in a long time, and he was surprised by this.

The book was about the Sargasso Sea. A man had survived a sinking. He was adrift on an inflatable raft. This man had been crossing the Atlantic on an eighty-foot private yacht when it went down. He had been a guest on this crossing, and had not wanted to go, but because of problems at home, he agreed to come along. In a storm at night, a wave, taller than the ship itself, swept it onto its side, and he had found a raft and got it into the water, and climbed on. During the night he called to his friends and the ones still alive called to him, but he never found them, and in the morning he was alone.

While floating on the raft, he came upon a ghost ship. The ship was empty. It was sitting calmly in the water at the edge of the Sargasso Sea. The man used a cable hanging from the ghost ship to climb aboard. It was empty, but sound and afloat. That was why it was called a ghost ship. Seamen feared a ship like this, and would not board her. The man in the raft was glad for the safety of the ship, and climbed on.

There were provisions on this ship, and fresh water in sealed jars. The ship, with now the one man on board, drifted farther into the Sargasso Sea.

As Monroe read, Ronnie first lay against the back of the couch, and then his shoulder, and then put her head on his lap, under the book, and stretched her legs and propped them on the armrest. When he stopped reading and looked down at her, she thought. Yes. Do it now. Kiss me now.

He did. He leaned over and kissed her, and he made his mouth fit perfectly to hers, and he held his lips against hers for a longer than usual time for a kiss, an afternoon kiss, a first kiss, and when he lifted away from her, her lips seemed to come with him, to follow him up, and they remained in the same shape they'd become while he was kissing her, open, parted, and a mirror of his own.

It was quiet after that. There was only the creak of the couch, like the creak of a ship at sea, as it rolled in the swells, or rubbed against the wharf, rising and falling from the wash of other ships passing by, just the creak of the wood frame against the wall behind the couch, the legs against the floor, as if at sea.

"I knew it would be like that," Ronnie said.

"We shouldn't have done that," Monroe said.

"It was just a kiss. Just what I wanted. That is not so bad."

"It was bad enough," he said.

"It was good enough," she said.

"It was wrong."

"It was just right."

"It may have felt just right, but it cannot happen again."

"It can't?"

"No."

"But it should. It could."

"No."

"It might," she said.

"It cannot be. You may visit, like you have been, but we cannot go any further. We can't."

Ronnie went home. The phone rang. It was Monroe's friend from the hospital. It was the doctor who often worked the same shift as he. He began to tell him about a patient. The patient was a woman. She was self-admitted. That is, she arrived by herself, filled out her own forms, and waited to be seen.

"Buddy, old buddy," the doctor said, "I wish

you'd been here. This poor old gal's boyfriend attacked her in a jealous fit, and glued a patch of nylon, a heavy grade of nylon, like in a parachute, right between her legs. Right over everything. She was mortified, to say the least."

"He glued it?" Monroe asked.

"With Krazy Glue. She said he thought she'd been sleeping with other men."

MARTHA AND BOB WERE to visit that evening.
Monroe cleaned the house. Lydia finished work. She
came home. There was no evidence of the kiss.

"I am tired," she said. "Really tired."

"Take it easy, then. The house is clean, everything's ready."

"I wish they weren't coming tonight. Bob can be
such a jerk."

"It's of no consequence. He doesn't matter to us."

"Still, I don't like to be around him. He makes
fun of everything. Puts everyone down. Remember
when he lit in on you for going to school where you
did, and then just working in the ER?"

"I ignored it."

"He seemed to think there was something wrong
with going to such a grand school, and then doing
what you do."

"He's entitled to his opinion."

"I hope Martha leaves him. Someday, I'll tell you
the whole story. All of it."

Shortly after seven, Bob and Monroe left to get

beer and pizza. The pizza they wanted was across town. It took some time to get there. Lydia and Martha talked.

"What happened to your lip, anyway?" Lydia asked.

"I bit it."

"You bit your own lip?"

"I slammed on brakes, and I bit into it."

"Oh. Well, finish telling me about Earl."

"He's my best student. He wants to learn everything. He tries hard. And, he's incredibly good-looking."

"Now I see. Now I get it."

"He's big and rough looking. But not rough, like mean, but more like rugged. But he's gentle as a lamb, inside."

"What's he in for?"

"I don't know. Some kind of minor drug thing, and some other baloney about petty larceny."

"That doesn't sound too good."

"I know it doesn't, but he didn't do any of it. He told me all about it. The cops framed him. They planted drugs on him, so they could bust him."

"But why? Why would they do that?"

"Because they do it all the time."

"To who? They do it to who all the time?"

"All kinds of people. See, this is something no one knows about in this country, but people like Earl and some of his friends are political prisoners."

"Oh, come on, Martha. You don't believe that, do you?"

"Yes, I believe it. People who go against the system, like, you know, deal in marijuana, or grow it, or whatever, not that Earl did any of that, but people who do things like that, see, when you've got these

liquor companies and cigarette companies controlling
the system, then the cops, who are like agents for
these liquor companies and stuff, they bust you for
anything. It's politics, see. Just politics. That's why
Earl calls himself a political prisoner."

"I'm sorry, Martha, but it sounds like nonsense to
me."

"It's not nonsense, and when you meet Earl, and
have him explain it to you, you'll understand it, too."

"Okay. Okay. I'm glad you're happy, and that's
what's important to me, and if you want to believe in
political prisoners, go ahead."

"I will. And I'll believe in Earl, too."

"Good. You believe in Earl, and I'll believe in all
the things I need to believe in."

IT WAS A warm night. Monroe had bought the beer,
so Bob went in for the pizza, and Monroe leaned
against the building. They were the only white people
as far as he could see in any direction.

The building across from him was to be demol-
ished. It was three stories high. A crane with a
wrecking ball was parked in front. Some boys played
on the crane, and swung from the cable holding the
ball. More boys were inside the cab, pulling on the
levers and making the sounds of the engine and what
the building would do when it crashed down.

A man and a woman approached Monroe. The
man walked slightly in front of the woman. Her face
was turned away from him. The woman was on a
leash. The man held the leash in his right hand. It was
a dog leash. It had a snap coupler on the end. The
snap was attached to a link in a lightweight chain
around the woman's neck.

As they approached, other people passed them,

and some of them spoke to the man, and nodded at the woman. The woman on the leash evidently lived with this man, and the neighborhood people knew them.

They stopped two stores away from the pizza parlor. The man tied the woman to an iron grate that protected the plate-glass window. He went inside. The woman remained still. She did not look unhappy. It wasn't as if he never took her anywhere.

"What are you staring at?" Bob asked.

"Nothing."

"Let's get out of here, then. This place is not safe."

"You're right," Monroe said.

Across the street, as the two white men drove off, one of the boys found the key. He started the crane. He found the lever that worked the winch that controlled the boom. He swung the ball and slammed it into the building. It did less than everyone thought. It knocked a hole in the masonry only the size of the ball itself.

This made the boy mad. He swung the ball farther back this time, to get a running start. A crowd of people came to watch. The boy slammed the iron ball into the wall again, and this time a whole section came away with it.

Then the man who owned the woman chained to the railing returned. He unhooked her and walked her back down the street. In his hand was a box of fried chicken. The box was called the Snacker-Packer. It was meant for two people to share. Inside it were four pieces of chicken, two biscuits, and two cups of slaw.

"SPEAKING OF BELIEVING in things, sort of along the line of hearing things, listen to this," Lydia told Martha while they waited for the men to return. "Last weekend, after that night I went out of control trying to get Monroe to talk to me, you know?"

"Yes. I remember," Martha said.

"Well, later that night, he didn't want to make love, and I got mad, and yelled at him, you mean I'm going to have to give up sex for the rest of my life?"

"What'd he do?"

"Nothing. Just withdrew further."

"You need to lighten up, girl."

"I know, but he drives me crazy. I mean, good crazy and bad crazy. He's so attractive to me. I find myself doing and saying things I know I shouldn't do or say the very minute I do them. But the reason I started telling you this is that, like believing in things that might not be there, you can get so bad off you hear things that might not be there, also.

"The other night, we were sitting on a couch and he was reading an article and I asked, what's that, and he folded a page to the title and said, without looking at me, clitoral drift."

"Oh, come on, Lydia. Did he say that?"

"He did. I swear he did."

"Well, what is it?"

"That's what I wanted to know. It could have been anything. Those medical journals have everything you *never* wanted to know in them, so, I thought for a while, and decided it was some sort of sexual dysfunction, and I kept thinking about it while he calmly read this article about it, and finally I said, Monroe, what *is* clitoral drift?"

"And?"

"And he put down the magazine and looked at me like I was totally out of it, and said, Lydia, I have no earthly idea, and when he said that, I grabbed the magazine from him and turned back to the title page, and, wouldn't you know it, the blasted article was about literal, or lateral drift, or something like that, to do with geology."

"Oh my."

"There I was and there he was. He was reading about geology. I was sitting beside him going bananas from not being paid attention to, and he's reading geology."

"You've got to relax, girl."

"I know. I just need some attention. I go cuckoo sometimes, when I get ignored. Later, though, I was thinking more about it, and I decided I did have clitoral drift myself. I decided it was something you get when your husband or boyfriend won't pay any attention to you."

"Lydia."

"I'm going to write an article for the medical magazines about it, to help the doctors' wives who have husbands who sit beside them reading geology or pharmaceutical journals, while they go into the drift state."

NEXT DOOR, MR. Cutler and Mrs. Cutler and Ronnie were summoned to the table. They were summoned by the ringing of a bell. The bell was sterling silver and delicate. The person ringing the bell was named Arkansas, and she was their maid.

The Cutlers had inherited Arkansas, along with her husband, Ernest, who did the yard work, when they inherited the house. Arkansas and Ernest were in their eighties, and were the last of the old-time Negroes in town.

"Is yo want yo food now?" she asked. Arkansas could talk better than that, but she slipped into dialect when she was at work because it made Mrs. Cutler so happy.

"Yes, we are ready," she said. Ye-us, we aah ray-dee." Mrs. Cutler liked to get high and mighty with her accent, herself.

They were served veal. Ronnie could not eat it. She could not look at it. The veal was the color, almost precisely, of her mother's skin. Besides the color, the meat on her plate had fine lines of ligaments and tendons in it, and the lines looked like the marks in her mother's skin, where it folded in on itself.

Her mother was famished. There'd been a long wait after the meal was ready, and Arkansas rang the bell for everyone to come to the table, because no one could locate Mrs. Cutler, and after a search by Ronnie, Arkansas, and Mr. Cutler, which included the backyard, up and down the street, and even the shed attached to the garage, Arkansas finally found her in the closet in her upstairs bedroom. Arkansas had come downstairs after she found her, and looked at Mr. Cutler and motioned with her head toward the room upstairs, and tipped her hand to her mouth, as if she were holding a bottle, and said, "Yeah, she up there all right. She done found a new place to hide it."

Mrs. Cutler then, with little but liquid in her stomach all day, was starved, and when her plate was set in front of her, she wrapped one arm around it, to hold it steady, and ate voraciously with her free hand.

She pulled the plate close to her. Her huge arm folded over it and held it as tightly as it could without breaking it. In a hurry to get down the food, and having no time to switch back and forth to the knife, and having no free hand to do that, she used the side of the fork when she had to cut anything.

As Ronnie could not look at her own plate, and could not look at her father's, which had the same cut of meat, she stared straight ahead and tried to ignore her mother tearing into her food. Try as she might, she could see, out of the corner of her eyes; and as she watched, she saw her mother, in a frenzy to get something else onto her fork and into her mouth, cut a chunk of flesh out of her own arm, the one wrapped around the plate, and stuff the chunk into her mouth.

"Oh no," Ronnie gasped.

"Eat everything on your plate, Veronica," her mother said, "or you'll get nothing to eat the rest of the night. Do you hear me?"

Ronnie looked down and nodded.

"Look at me when I talk to you," she said, and Ronnie did, and saw her mother chewing her food and talking at the same time, and watched everything rolling around inside her mouth like a load of clothes inside a washing machine, and she could also see the piece of her mother's arm tumbling over and over, until she went into the rinse cycle, and washed everything down with a glass of water.

"STILL," LYDIA SAID, on the porch with Martha and waiting for the men to return, "sometimes you have to take hold of these men and tie them down in a chair and make them talk to you. They won't ever tell you what they're thinking unless you do."

"I never wanted to know," Martha said.

"I'm working hard on this guy. I want it to work. He's good. He's good inside. He's smart, handsome, and good-hearted. It's up to me, is all, to access it."

"I don't know, Lydia."

"He's going to talk to me tonight, or else. I'm going to force it out of him, if I have to squeeze him like a mop."

"You better think twice about that."

"I've thought more than twice. Once they finally

talk to you, everything's much better. It's worth the temporary hell of the fight."

THE FIGHT CAME early.

"You know what you did just now?" Lydia asked after their friends had left and she saw a good moment to confront him.

"What, sweetie. What did I do?"

"You did that maddening thing of acting like everything is hunky-dory in front of people, even when you know it isn't."

"I thought everything was."

"Boy, that makes me mad. You ought to have the decency to make up with me before you go faking everything with everybody else."

"I think you should go to bed. Have some water first, though. As much as you can stand to drink. The dehydrating effect of the alcohol is what gives that morning-after feeling."

"I'm not drunk."

"I think you might be."

"Don't tell me what I am and am not."

"I didn't say what you weren't. Just what you were. Are."

"Sit down here a minute," she said, and steered him into a chair. "You know, you don't have to pretend to love me if you don't. A woman can tell. You hardly pay any attention to me anymore."

"That's untrue, Lydia."

"You probably thought when you started dating me, well, you thought I'll just have a fling with this little clerk in the back room, and that'll be it."

"I never thought that."

"I know I'm not supposed to mention Katy," she said, and then covered her mouth and looked

wide-eyed. "Oh my, I said her name. The unmention-
able name of THE FIRST WIFE, the name itself of
THE LOVE OF YOUR LIFE."

"Leave her out of this," he said, and covered his
face and rubbed his skin, trying to shake off the effects
of not only a terribly long day, but the memory of
Katy, as well.

"But I can tell things, you know. I've been loved
before. And dearly so. Passionately so. At least I
was loved, which is something you may not have
known."

"All right, Lydia. Have it your way."

"He loved me, you know, even if he didn't know
how to show it."

"I'm certain he did."

"He loved me, even if I let him think he didn't,
which I hate myself for, but he did."

"That's wonderful."

"He loved me, even if he forgot he did."

"Then you should have stayed with him. I didn't
ask you to leave."

"You did so."

"I did not. You begged me to take you in."

"OH, YOU LIAR," she screamed. "You rotten
liar. I never did that."

"Nope. I guess not. I guess I dreamed it."

"You dreamed it, is right. The idea of begging you
for anything makes me ill."

"Go be ill in the bathroom. You'll feel better afterward."

"I'm not sick."

"Go to bed, Lydia. Everything's okay. You're fine.
I'm fine. We're fine. You're drunk. Go sleep it off."

"No."

"I have nothing more to say, then."

"We used to sit on this couch and laugh and carry on just nonstop."

"We still do."

"We don't."

"We do."

"Then why not now?"

"Because you're drunk."

"I'm not, and you're going to tell me what's been wrong with you, or us, lately, or you will not get one minute's sleep the rest of this night. You hear?"

"Back off, a little. Maybe you could get what you wanted if you just gave a fellow some room."

"Oh, you want some room? Is that it?"

"A little."

"I'll give you all the room you want."

"Don't go overboard."

"But that's the way I am. That's the way I was when you, quote, fell in love with me, unquote. Right?"

"It won't work. I'm not going to fight with you. It simply won't work."

"I'll not leave this room, and you won't, either, until you tell me what I did that you didn't like."

"Oh, I will leave this room. As a matter of fact, I will take a little walk outside and get some air, and when I return, let's relax and call an end to this long day."

"Don't even try to walk out that door."

"Move, please," he said.

"No."

"Move out of the way, please."

"I'm not going to bed another night with whatever it is that's keeping us apart."

"Stop, Lydia. I'm trying to be nice about this, but it won't last. You're about to push me too far."

"Push you? Like this?" she said, and shoved him backwards.

"I'm going out that door, Lydia. Just step aside."

"You will not leave this house. It's that simple."

He walked around her. She moved with him. When he took a step toward the front of the house, she took that same step. He stepped to one side, and she did, and when she did, he ran past her toward the front door. As he reached it, she caught up to him, and flung herself in front of him. She blocked the door. She backed against it, and put her hips against the knob, and spread her arms and legs across the width of the door.

"Don't try it," she said.

"Move, Lydia."

"Don't try it."

"You're out of control. You need to stop."

"You need to stop."

"I'll go out the back, then," he said.

She grabbed him. She held him right where he was.

"Let go of me," he said.

"I will when you do what you should do."

"I'm warning you," he said. "You're going to get hurt."

"I dare you. I dare you to lay a hand on me."

"You better let go."

"Go ahead and hit me, then, you coward. Afraid to talk. Afraid to do anything. Go ahead. I dare you."

It was hard to resist. Had Monroe not seen men and women who'd beat each other half to death or knifed each other or shot each other, had it not been for all of that, and the remorse they brought with them, how sorry they seemed once it was over, he would have grabbed her and hurt her. He would have slung her across the room and kicked her in the face. But he did not.

"No, Lydia. I won't. It's not that I'm afraid, actually. It's more that I don't want to get down to your level."

He went to the back of the house. She followed him, and when he went out the back and into the yard, she grabbed him by the arm and spun him around.

Next door, from her second-floor bedroom window, Ronnie was leaning out into the night, listening and watching.

"Come back in the house," Lydia said.

"I'm going to take a walk. Then I'll come back in and we'll talk. Maybe."

Lydia watched him walk away. If felt bad to her. It felt much worse than it actually was. It felt like all the men she'd ever let walk out on her, walk over her. It felt like watching her father walk out on her mother. It felt like the frustration and infuriating helplessness of all of those things.

"I HATE YOU," she screamed.

She screamed so loud that Monroe, almost out of the yard, turned around, but he kept walking, and tripped over his own feet, and by the time he hit the ground, Lydia was on top of him, holding him by the hair, and once more screaming into his face.

"I HATE YOU. YOU JERK."

Monroe struggled with Lydia to get her hands out of his hair, and in the middle of the struggle, without realizing it clearly, both he and Lydia became aware of someone else's voice.

"I said git up."

They stopped fighting, and they both looked above them and saw Ronnie standing over them with a pistol in her hand.

"Now git up, you sidewinder," she said, and shoved Lydia with her foot so that Lydia fell off Monroe and onto the grass.

Lydia stood up, and Monroe did the same.

"Now, reach for the sky," Ronnie said, pointing the gun at Lydia, "or I'll turn you into Swiss cheese."

"Put down the gun, Ronnie," Monroe said.

"I ain't a-gonna hurt you none," she said, and waved him away with her free hand.

"Put it down anyway," he said.

Lydia had her hands way up, reaching for the dark sky above her.

"Give it to me," he said, and walked toward her.

"Aw shucks," Ronnie said, and tossed him the gun, "it ain't real." He caught the plastic gun in the air, and Ronnie ran past him, and out of the yard, and back to her house.

"You can put your hands down now," Monroe said to Lydia.

She dropped her hands to her sides, and they walked into the house.

"I've never had a gun pointed at me before," she said.

"It's just a plastic replica," he said and gave it to her.

They went in the kitchen. Lydia took out a bottle of wine, and she shakily poured each of them a glass. They drank, and they talked, standing at the counters across from each other.

"I'm sorry," she said.

He nodded.

"Do you forgive me?" she asked.

"Sure."

"Do you understand why I got so upset?"

"I guess."

During the time they had walked in together, and she was pouring the wine, and had handed him the glass, she felt like he was back with her, and things were all right again. But as she began to talk to him again, he seemed to withdraw once more, to fade away, to go into himself.

"You don't understand, do you?" she asked.

"Yes. I understand. People get upset. It's the way it is with people, and always will be."

"But there are reasons people get upset. That's what I want you to understand. What they are."

He sipped his wine. He turned away from her. He looked out the dark window toward Ronnie's house.

"I thought things were okay between us," he said.

"No, they're not, and you know they're not."

"How would I know that?" he said to her suddenly, and with a different voice. "How? You see, that is a complex conclusion, and not a simple one, and not the sort of conclusion one would draw easily without thinking carefully on it, and so, sure, things are okay if I say they are, and, at the same time, they're not okay if you say they're not, and both of us are right, because it's all in one's mind, really."

"Why are you talking to me this way?" she asked.

"I'm talking to you this way to try to get you to understand that the answer to the question, are we okay, is not as simple as someone as simple as you would like it to be. It involves perceptions, beliefs, expectations, and the whole range of unspoken promises concerning the contracts between men and women that have existed since the beginning of the modern era. The answer involves roles and the evolution of said roles, all things like that, what men mean to women, and what women mean to men, those types of beliefs, deep-seated, intrinsic to the character of the person or persons involved, and, I might add, difficult to see in another person, quite difficult, indeed, I should say, so, when you take those complexities into account, the answer to your question is likely better left unanswered, unspoken. Got it?"

"Yeah, I got it," she said. "I got a headache full of bullshit, and what I want to know is, simply put from this simple person, do you love me, or don't you?"

"Sure," he said, looking at his watch. "I love you."

"You don't sound like it. Your voice doesn't sound like it."

"Sorry about that," he said, and looked at his watch again, "but I'm tired, and I probably sound tired because I am tired, and I think, if you will allow it, I'll go to bed."

He started past her on his way out of the room.

"Kiss me, then, and let's really make up," she said, "before we keel over from exhaustion."

"I'm too tired for anything," he said.

"Too tired for a kiss?"

He pecked her on her cheek.

"I'm going upstairs to bed."

"You mean you won't even sleep in the same bed with me?" she asked.

"Not tonight. I'm going upstairs."

"But please, baby. I'm sorry if I got too upset. I just got frustrated. Please come on and go to bed with me. We don't have to do anything. Just cuddle."

She went to the double bed alone. She lay down. She fell asleep immediately, but then awoke just as quickly. She tossed around. At first, she was trying to get comfortable. Then, as she heard how much noise the bed and frame made with her tossing and turning, she did more of it, so he would hear her.

She wanted the bed to come apart. She wanted the bed to fall apart, and the mattress to crash to the floor, and the springs pop out, and the headboard slam back against the wall, and the sheets tear and rip, and she wanted to fall into all of it, and cling to the boards with her fingers and her nails, which would screech like chalk on a blackboard, and which he would hear and would feel to him like a fork dragging through his teeth, and he might come down and see her, see what he'd done to her, see what had happened. She ought to do that and he ought to come down and see. He should. He just should.

8

BOB WAS AWAKE. HE could hear Martha. He thought the pizza had been bad, or the beer. Maybe she couldn't sleep because she was changing so, like a teenager growing up. She had certainly changed. She almost looked good. She carried herself differently. The thinner she got, the taller she looked.

The light was on from her room. He listened at the door. He could hear sounds like scratching or rubbing. There was a mysterious, rhythmic quality, and he could not understand what she was doing.

He went outside. It was a warm night. The stars were out. He crept around to the side of the house. Her bedroom window faced the woods. The window was open. He had to be quiet. The dog looked at him. Bob put his finger to his lips and the dog looked away.

Her shade was up and her curtains were back and a breeze flowed in. She was sitting up in bed. Her legs were bare. Her nightgown had slid to her hips. Her legs were the first thing he saw as he crept around the house.

She had an artist's sketchbook in her lap. She was drawing a man's head. Beside her were a few earlier attempts. The steady sound he'd heard was the charcoal on the paper as she dabbed in the lines of the hair, the skin, the texture.

He hated her. She was more stupid than the dog under the porch. The dog had enough sense to know when it was not wanted. She did not. She had hung around for years, as if she could not take a hint. Far be it from him to leave. It would never have looked right.

Couldn't she take a hint? How many hints, how many more, could he give? She was more stupid than the dog under the porch.

She straddled the tablet. It was so late at night. What kind of person would be sitting up in bed drawing pictures? What kind of person? What kind of woman? What kind of wife? A stupid one. A crazy one. A menopausal madam, with a post-periodic, pouting pudenda, he told himself, and then smiled at his own alliterative and poetic abilities. He was rather, more than rather, shall we say, quite, yes, that's the word, quite proud of how quickly he put that little phrase together.

She annoyed him so, he suddenly yelled, loudly.

"Ahhhhh!" he screamed.

She looked. She could not see in the dark. She knew who it was.

It would have been embarrassing, yes, quite, if any of his literature students had seen him howling in the yard at his ex-wife wife. It would have looked bad. Thank goodness there were places you could do a bit of howling, and run around slightly mad, and no one, who mattered, would see it.

———

IN THE COUNTY prison unit, Earl was awake. The lights were off. The lights were centrally controlled. The exits were lit, and, along the corridor, every fourth light remained on, but in a dimmer than usual mode. Earl had the bottom bunk. The dominant inmate had the bottom bunk.

"You're crude," he told his roommate Selby. "And women don't like men that way."

"I know whats women like, and whats they don't. You don't have to tell me."

"Take Martha, for instance."

"Yeah, I'd take her. Right now," he said.

"The reason she likes me, and not you, is refinement. That's the reason," Earl told him.

"I could do some refining on her, right now, as a matter of fact."

"You need to study. You need to read more. You need to expand your horizons," Earl said.

"I've done expanded all I can get right now," he said.

"You need to learn to respect women," Earl said.

"I respect them," Selby told him. "Especially in bed."

"Women are different from men."

"Man, are they ever."

"God made them different from the menfolk," Earl said.

"And I thank Him for it every day. I'm about to thank Him right now," Selby said.

"You're crude, Selby. You've got one thing on your mind. You've got to learn to control yourself."

"Right."

"You need to meet someone like Martha. She'd change you. She's different."

"I like them different myself. Chinese, Swedish massage, any of them's all right with me."

"I'll be glad to get out of here. I'm a new man," Earl said, "and Martha's the reason."

RONNIE WENT OUT the back door. She ran down the street. She saw a light in Monroe's house. The light was upstairs and the rest of the house was dark. Hey. Hey, you. She called to him, but he would never have heard that far away.

A car turned down the street. She hid. The car passed. It was the police. They patrolled this time of night along her street regularly. She often saw them. They never saw her.

After she ambled down the street, she cut through a yard and passed a group of animals that were gathered under an old concrete birdbath, and then ran all the way to a small shopping center where a convenience store was open twenty-four hours a day. The woman behind the counter was dark-skinned. She had fine features. She was from Pakistan. Because people from Pakistan had never lived in this part of the South before, the rednecks did not know what she was, and assumed she was a nigger. Ronnie liked her.

"Hi," Ronnie said.

"Hello."

Ronnie loved to hear her talk. She loved the singsong rhythm of the words, and the colorful dot above her eyes, and the fine bones in her hands, and the slow and deliberate and courteous manner in which she did things.

"I couldn't sleep."

"Many people come in here saying the same thing."

"Sometimes I sleep well. I hit the bed, and bam.

I'm out. Sometimes, though, I fall asleep right away, and then, just as quickly, wake up."

"Yes."

"When I do that, I can't go back."

"It is dangerous for you to walk around this time of night, is it not?"

"No. Not for me. I can outrun anybody."

"Oh, yes?"

She bought a candy bar. She ate it while looking through a magazine. A young man drove up. The car he was driving was an old, beat-up Ford Pinto. The top had been cut open as if the man had intended to put in a sunroof but had never gotten any further than the hole.

The car was painted wild colors, and the man driving was so thin he looked as if he weighed less than a ten-year-old child, and the bones in his face were like rocks pushing out through his cheeks.

"Hey, babe," he said to Ronnie.

"Hey, babe," she said back.

"Do you want to go for a ride?"

"Nope."

"Are you sure?"

"Yes."

"All right. Stay cool, hot stuff," he said, and bought a pack of cigarettes. Just before he left the lot, his hand appeared out the hole in the roof, and the cellophane wrapper from the cigarette pack floated into the air.

"He was not your type?" the clerk asked in a joking way.

"No. I have a boyfriend already."

Then the man in the Pinto came back down the street. He had the car wound out all the way in first gear so that the motor was roaring, but the car itself was only traveling about thirty miles an hour. As he passed, he jerked upright in his seat so that his head popped up through the roof of the car, through the hole. With his long, skinny neck and the wicked, wide-eyed grin on his face, he looked like the clownish head of a jack-in-the-box unexpectedly popping up right at you.

"Durn fool," Ronnie said, and bought another candy bar and a small bottle of apple juice and left the store. She took a shortcut home, and passed a house that sat alone in the middle of the trees in the ravine across from where she lived. She skirted it, along a path she knew, and ran back into her room.

"I BLEW IT," LYDIA told Martha when she called her at lunch, which was the time they had arranged to get in touch with each other. "I made a mess of things. I thought it was going to work, but it didn't. Obviously, it did not. I'll figure something else out."

"Good idea."

"A lot of times with men, you do have to push them a little to get them to see themselves. It's worked before."

"You two'll be okay."

"I feel better anyway. Getting real mad sometimes makes you feel better, even if nothing changes."

"Maybe."

"Changes for the better, I mean. He's changed, all right, but for the worse. Like with clothes. I got ready to wear something great today, and then I didn't have the nerve because I could just see the look that was going to cross his face, or, rather, the look that says, I see nothing, I feel nothing, you're nothing."

"I hate that."

"I just got these new clothes, which he used to

love, especially that Mexican-looking dress I got at the fancy used-clothing store, and now I've got no one to wear it for."

"Wear it for yourself," Martha said.

"I do, but it's not as much fun."

"It's something we've got to learn."

"What?"

"Doing for ourselves."

"Oh, yeah. But it's kind of like sex. It's not nearly as much fun by yourself."

"Right."

"It is the sex, you know," Lydia continued. "Whenever you finally find the right man and suddenly the sex is so good it's like the kind of sex and love and intimacy you've only read about or heard about, and suddenly, you've got it, then, I tell you, Martha, you just don't want to let it go."

"I bet."

"Remember that time I told you about when Marcus and I were splitting up, and we hadn't made love in a long time, and he was worried and mad and tense and stuff like that, and then finally, we did it. Did I tell you about that?"

"I think so. What happened?"

"Well, it just went on and on and on. He couldn't finish, you know. I thought I would go mad. I couldn't breathe. It was like he was breathing up all the air in the room. It was awful. Really awful."

"I've been there myself."

"That was the last time we ever made love."

"A bad time."

"But anyway, how did I get off onto that?"

"Good sex."

"Right. With Monroe. You see, it's just unbelievable. It's so good, it's unreal. It's like our skin's got something that goes electric, or whatever, when we touch."

"Lucky you."

"I know. I know that. That's why I know it's right between us. A good man is hard to find."

"So I've heard."

"I mean a man with a good heart, a good soul, who's right for you."

MONROE CLEANED THE upstairs bathroom, which was seldom used. He sprinkled bleaching powder on the various porcelain fixtures, and then sat on the floor, leaning against the side of the tub, while the solution soaked in. He remembered two boys, two teenage boys, who came into the emergency room a few months ago. The boys had been at a restaurant, the police report said. They had been with some other boys. All of the boys went into the bathroom. In this bathroom was one urinal, one sink, and one stall with a toilet inside.

There was a man in the stall. The stall was in the middle of the room. According to the report, the boys wanted to use the stall, but the man was still seated. The boys climbed on the stall, and peered over the top at him, and made faces and laughed at him. They harassed him mercilessly. They beat on the sides of the stall. They threw paper towels over the top.

The boys bammed on the sides of the stall until it sounded to the man as if the walls were going to fall on him, and they kept climbing up and down, and peering at him and laughing and throwing things.

The man was trapped in the most humiliating situation of his life, and evidently he had not liked it. When he came out, he stuck a knife in two of the boys and would have injured the others except they ran out the door. The boys thought what they were doing was funny and, until the knife appeared, were laughing hysterically. Then the man stuck the knife in them. It went in, and came back out, without a sound. When it came out, blood followed the blade, and little pieces of tissue and organ flowed out the wound. Suddenly, it was not funny anymore.

The thing that interested Monroe was how one thing could be so absolutely, uncontrollably funny and innocent to one person, and how it could be so absolutely horrible and malevolent to another. It was like that all the time in the emergency room. People entered wounded, having received the assault, they would insist, without provocation. Whatever they'd been doing, they had not known it was doing something different, vastly different, to the other person.

An older man came in during Monroe's shift recently. He was wheeled past Monroe. As he passed, he rose up and grasped Monroe's hand. Monroe, he called. Monroe had not recognized him. This man was a doctor, himself. He was a specialist. He was sixty years old. His wife had beaten him with a baseball bat while he slept. She thought he'd been unfaithful to her. He said he had not. He did say he'd thought about it. He did admit to thinking about it. But he said he had not.

Sometimes it only took thinking about it. She'd beat him so badly his head swelled beyond its normal size. Monroe had not even recognized him. They were both grandparents. The grandkids loved them. They called the woman who had beaten him with the bat, Gram-Gram.

The old doctor had to leave town. The wife left town. She moved south, to the coast, and he went north. One night. One awful night. It could happen to anyone. People had to be careful. He saw the ones who had not been careful. It seemed an easy thing to do, to make a mistake about another person.

Later that day, Monroe found the book he'd been reading. He settled into the chaise lounge Lydia had angrily occupied the night before. Ronnie saw him and ran out the door and through the hedge and right up to him.

"Hello."

"That was some fight last night," she said. She paced around while she talked.

"You saw it all?"

"Sure."

"You mean you were in the backyard watching?"

"No. Not exactly. First I watched from my room, and then I came down."

"I wish you had not."

She climbed onto the arms of one of the chairs, and stood on them, one leg on each, and balanced with her hands out to her sides.

"You're no good, you know."

"I'm not. At what?" he asked.

"At fighting. You should have decked her. She was asking for it."

"I wouldn't do that."

"I would have. I almost did it for you."

He tossed her the plastic gun. She caught it with one hand then jumped into the air and landed on the seat cushions in a sitting position, like a gymnast on a trampoline.

"Be careful, Ronnie. You'll break the chair. This is not our furniture."

"She's tough. I think she's pretty tough. But I could take her."

"Stay out of it, all right?"

"I'm a lot tougher than I look. My muscles are really, really strong."

"I'm sure of that, but one doesn't attack someone else, just out of the blue."

"She did you."

"That's different. That's somewhat more complex."

"I am awesome at full speed. You should see me run."

"I have seen you."

"Not full blast. I believe I could run as fast as a horse. I do. If I really got rolling and got my rhythm right, I believe I could outrun a horse."

"No, you couldn't, Ronnie. No human could."

"I could," she said, and pumped her legs up and down as if limbering up for a race. "Do you jog?"

"I have. But not for some time."

"You should."

"True. I should. Releases endomorphins. I could use that."

"We could run outside. Do you want to? I'll let you win."

"Not now."

"What do you want to do?"

"I was reading my book."

"Read to me, then. I want to find out what happens."

He read.

The shipwrecked man in the ghost ship floated into the clump of other ships within the Sargasso Sea. The ships were close together, and the currents, moving in a slow, terminal ever inward whorl, kept them against one another. He could climb up, or jump down, to them.

There were sealed provisions on many of the ships.

He scouted a place to set up housekeeping. While he did, the ships turned slowly, around and around, a revolution a day, but remained geographically in the same spot.

Soon, a new ship drifted in. This was the first new ship the man had seen drawn into the hundreds of others that were there. He watched it come closer.

It took a day. Time was nothing. There was plenty to eat. There was little else to do. Finally, the new ship touched another, and the stranded man climbed from ship to ship until he found a way on board.

The man searched the cabins. In one there was a passenger. The passenger was a woman, and she was nearly dead. She was dehydrated, and must have been knocked unconscious when whatever happened to the ship caused everyone to abandon it. There was a gash in the side of her head, and the blood around the gash had dried in her hair.

Her face was battered. Her clothes were ripped. Her skirt was torn. She could not talk. The man brought her water. She choked on it. Finally, she was able to drink. She drifted in and out of consciousness. The man covered her with a blanket, and lay beside her. He put his arm across her, and rested his hand against her cheek, and patted her.

The ships went in a circle. In the water, the Sargasso weed moved in the same tedious whorl along with the ships. Around and around. Everything went around at the same speed, in the same direction, ever inward, bunching closer.

At the center were the oldest vessels. Some of them were wood, ancient galleons. As the ships congregated from the center outward, they reflected the passing of time, from a certain beginning, to the time of this man, and now this woman, injured, battered, weak, and in his care.

While Monroe read to Ronnie, she walked back and forth in front of him, watching him sometimes, twirling the gun, and then, quickly looking away, and then walking back again from the other direction, and unexpectedly looking at him again, as if she were trying to catch him at something, or figure something out, or about to tell him something, something, but couldn't.

"Do you ever sit still?" he asked.

"Not often," she said. She took out a soft, black rubber ball, a bit smaller than a tennis ball, and began to bounce it on the floor. He continued reading.

"Are you listening to the story?"

"Sure. He's looking for a place to live. I'm listening. Keep going."

Soon Ronnie perched in a chair. She bounced the ball between her legs for awhile, and then threw it across the room, against the wall, let it bounce once on its way back to her, and then caught it. She did this again and again.

Finally, Monroe stopped reading and quietly watched her.

"Are you through?" she asked.

"Yes."

"Will you kiss me again?"

"No."

"Can we take a bath?"

"No."

"Okeydokey," she said, and ran out the back door.

In the time it took Ronnie to go out through his yard and into her own, but no longer, Monroe heard his front doorbell ring, and when he opened the door he saw Mrs. Cutler, who must have been lumbering up the steps to his house, but was unaware of Ronnie, who was going the other way, at the same time, but around back.

"Dr. Hopkins, I'm Laura Cutler, Veronica's mother." Doktah Hopkunz, Ahm Law-ra Cut-lah, Va-raw-ni-kus muthah.

"Yes," he said, and invited her in.

"Please excuse me for coming over like this without calling first, but I've noticed Veronica darting over here at times, and I wanted to be sure she wasn't making a nuisance of herself."

"Oh, she's not. Not at all. I enjoy her company."

"Well, that's good to hear, and I won't stay but a minute, but I did want to discuss with you, at your (at yo-ah) convenience, drawing on your knowledge in a professional way, in your office if you so prefer, any ideas you might have about Veronica, since you are getting to know her now, concerning her hyperactivity and what I'm sure you've discovered is her seeming detachment from reality, both of which we have had diagnosed in the past, but since we are doubly concerned about her now that she has become quite a woman, at least in her physical stature, any advice is most certainly appreciated."

"Mrs. Cutler, that's not my field, but I'd be happy to talk with you about Veronica anytime, casually, as neighbors, or any other way you desire."

"Well, maybe you and your wife could come over for supper some evening."

"That'd be wonderful. I'll mention it to Lydia."

"By the way," she said, and looked behind him, and scanned all the other rooms she could see from where she stood, "is my daughter here at the moment?"

"No. She's not. I think she went back home."

"Fine. Fine. Just so long as everything's all right. She's still an innocent child in many ways, you know."

She started out the front door.

"Now, you let me know if she bothers you, you hear?" she said, and was out the door, and gone, and as Monroe watched her walking back toward her own house, he heard, from an upstairs window next door, Ronnie bark like a dog just once, and then slam her window shut.

10

A PERSON RETURNS HOME. What has happened? In his absence, what has occurred? In her absence, what? Anyone might forget to tell even the most spectacular thing.

A plane flew over. It flew low. It crashed a mile away, only a few seconds in flight time. It could have hit the house, only its trajectory was not so steep, and it passed, and exploded and the bodies were burned and thrown through the air and stuck upright into the ground, like cactus plants.

You could forget to tell about a plane crash, or a visit, or a kiss. You could forget to tell anything if you wanted to.

"So, what'd you do?" Lydia asked, strong in her determination to be good, to do right, to leave him alone and quit worrying so much.

"Nothing," he said. "Just another day."

"Same here."

"I cleaned up a little."

"Thanks. Some men don't help out like that. I appreciate it."

"It's nothing. How was your day?"

"Pretty good. Even after last night. I hope we've both let that fade on into the past," she said.

"Sure, baby," he said, and hugged her. "That was last night, and this is now."

"I like that, living in the now. That's what they say we're supposed to do."

"Sounds right to me."

"The only thing is, on the way home my brakes didn't seem right. They haven't been right since I slammed them on to keep from hitting that dog."

"You need a new car."

"I know I need a new car, but I can't afford a new car."

"All you have to do is say the word, and I'll get it for you."

"I can't let you do that. You're sweet. You're so sweet to me, but I can't."

"I don't have anything to spend my money on," he said. "Just say the word."

"You're just too nice, sometimes. And after all I did, going so crazy last night."

"Forget it."

"And here I am, home late, again, and you have the courtesy not to even say anything about it."

"It's nothing."

"But it's been worth waiting for, let me tell you. Have I got some stories to tell you. I've been to see Martha, and listen to this," she said.

She told him about Martha's new apartment. Martha had left Bob. She'd moved into her own place.

"And guess what else?" she said, while they ate supper.

"What?"

"All the time they still lived together, they still made love."

"I would expect that."

"They still did it, even though he was sleeping around, and they had legally divorced, and all."

"That fits."

"I know, but listen to this. She told me that the whole time they made love, from the first year on, that Bob would not let her move."

"Move what?"

"I mean, when they made love, she had to lie there and be still. Not move at all."

"She told you that?"

"Yes."

"And she did it?"

"Yes."

"Hmmmmmmm," he said, thinking about it.

"You know how screwed up Martha's been. She said she didn't know why she did it, but that it wasn't that bad really."

"I see. Not that bad, huh?" he said, chuckled about it.

"She just lay there, she said, and he did his thing to her, and he'd make her be real still, and then, when he was finished, he'd leave the room, close the door, and go to sleep in his room."

"Sounds like fun."

"Sounds like real hell. But you know what? She said she was, at first, anyway, responsive, and used to get really excited, and then after he made her be still, just a few times, then it got to be every time, and he told her he enjoyed it more, because the way she used to be distracted him too much. It messed him up. Think about it, Monroe. Think about it."

"I am. I'd say he has some problems. No doubt about it."

"He'd have a problem if I'd been his wife, but anyway, I've been saving the best for last. Guess who her roommate is. Guess."

"I would have no way of knowing."

"It's Earl."

"You mean . . . ?"

"I mean the guy she's been teaching to cook in the prison. They had the whole thing planned. The day he was going to get out was the day she was going to leave Bob, and was also the day she and Earl were going to move into the apartment, which she had already rented and partly furnished."

"This does not sound good," Monroe said.

"And I met him."

"He was there?"

"Yes, Monroe. He lives there. I told you."

"I wonder if Bob knows."

"I doubt it. I doubt he knows what hit him yet."

"I hope he does not find out."

"That's what I thought all the while she's been telling me about him, but now that I've met him, I'm not sure he's so bad."

"You don't?"

"He's interesting. His life has been real hell. An abusive father, and his mother was sort of a prostitute, I mean, not entirely or professionally, but sort of."

"He told you all that?"

"No. Oh, no. Not him. Martha told me. But his life has been real hell, but it's like this magical thing has happened between him and Martha, and I think they're going to have a good life. I mean it."

"I wouldn't bet too heavily on it, Lydia."

"But he's actually really smart. He just needs a chance, and someone to care for him, and love him."

"Listen, Lydia. I see his kind all the time. I know what they look like, inside even."

"Well, it'd have to be the same. Everyone is the same inside, aren't they?"

"No."

"Well, anyway, he's not a criminal. He's just one of those guys who got put away, like a political prisoner type thing."

"Right, Lydia. Political prisoner. In America."

"Well, it's true. They arrested him for some phony charge, and planted drugs on him, and it was like the judge and everyone, the district attorney, were all in on it."

"Why would they do that, Lydia? Why?"

"Because, see, well, I'm not sure, really, but the way he told it, was very convincing. I believe him."

"I hope you're right."

"But the point of this event is that Martha has finally done something for herself and can live again now."

"Good. If that's true, then good. Maybe she won't have to lie still anymore."

"No way, baby. Not with this guy. It would be impossible."

"Poor old Bob. He is a jerk, and has his problems, but there's something about him I can almost understand. Something not entirely evil about him."

"Like what? Like nothing. I'm glad she left. And I hope he suffers the rest of his life."

"Maybe you're right. Their situation reminds me a bit of the little girl next door," he said.

"Who? The Cutlers' daughter?"

"Yes."

"What makes you think of her?"

"A life where a person seems to be trapped in a horrible situation with people who don't like her, or make her life hell when she doesn't seem to deserve it, or has done nothing to warrant it."

"How do you know all that? How do you know that about her?"

"I don't. I'm surmising. From watching her in the yard, and from watching her parents. There's something wrong over there, but I haven't figured out what, yet."

"You want me to find out for you?"

"No. That wouldn't work."

"I could find out. I've talked to the mother before."

"I think not."

"But, you see, I'd rather be the one to get involved, than have it be you. Understand?"

"Not entirely."

"You see, it occurred to me when you mentioned the little girl next door, I don't know what it was, your tone of voice, or the wistful look on your face, that this is what you did to me, this thing you have in you."

"What?"

"This thing where you feel sorry for someone, and you want to save them from something. Mostly women, I think."

"I'm not like that."

"Yes you are. It's a good thing, in a way, but it just hit me when you were talking about the girl, that it's what you did to me, too. You saved me. You rescued me. You helped me when I needed it so. I guess, damnit all, that you want to rescue her, too."

"No, that's not it."

"It is what you did to me, though. You found me in this dilapidated condition, and you rescued me. That's your whole trip, I guess. Now that I'm okay, you're bored with me. Right?"

"Wrong."

"No. I'm right. I'm afraid I am. Damnit all."

"Lydia, where did this suddenly come from and why?"

"From you. You started it when you told me about the new little waif you want to save."

"I didn't say anything about saving her."

"It's so strange. You're a doctor, but you don't know anything at all about yourself. Nothing. Nothing at all."

"And you do?"

"Do what? Know you, or me? What are you asking?"

"Forget it."

"I'm trying. Every day I try to forget all the things I don't want to remember. God knows I'm trying to."

"Now there's a place I might could help you," he said. "There are things like Prozac, Valium, and the like that might help you there."

"Oh, that's cute, Monroe. That's really cute."

"Just say the word."

"Oh heck," she said, and shook her head, as if admonishing herself. "I'm sorry. I don't know why I got off on that. I feel all stressed out. I don't know what it is. I'm worried, I guess. I'm just worried about things. I need to learn to keep my mouth shut. Let's just hug, okay. Let's just hug each other and be real quiet for a while, and just stand here and feel good, like we want to feel, like we ought to feel, okay? Let's just not talk for a while."

A few minutes later, they were sitting on the front

porch. There were few cars passing. It was an old neighborhood. The trees were as old or older than the houses, and towered above them. Lydia and Monroe leaned against the porch posts. Soon they became lost in their own thoughts.

Monroe, unexpectedly, began to remember a trip he took alone, before he met Lydia. It had been to Maine. He had once lived in Maine, when he was just out of college. He had lived there with Katy, his wife.

He had met Katy in college. She was at the top of her class. She had been planning to be a doctor for as long as she could remember. After she graduated, they took a year off, and it was during that year they moved to Maine, to a relative's farm in the middle of nowhere. Then, Monroe remembered, when they returned, Katy no longer wanted to go to medical school, and things started going bad. He never knew why.

This woman had been a great puzzle to Monroe. He had not understood her. He had not understood the way he acted with her. He had not known what to do with her. She had scared the hell out of him, he later figured out. Because he did not know what to do with her and because she puzzled him so much, he took off into the middle of Maine, to the middle of nowhere, and hid away with her.

This woman had been too good, too rich, in spirit, in beauty, in strength, in her love for him, in her commitment to life, their life, and life in general, too passionate, too fearless, and in retrospect, he thought, it must have scared the hell out of him.

Hiding away while he tried to figure out what to do with her, and with himself, had worked for a while. Then it did not work. For a while it was nice. It was sweet. It was romantic. Then it was not. For a while there was something unusual about them, about the way they lived, something special, something charmed, something pure and intimate and rare. It didn't last. They were doing things, though, while it did, that other people could not. They were living a way other people only thought about, but could not ever really do. Just the two of them. The rest of the world was far away, and corrupt, and unnecessary.

Then it went bad. She got sick. Maybe he made her sick. Maybe she got sick on her own. She stayed sick a long time. Everything changed.

Monroe, on the front porch now, with the new woman, this second woman in his life, not at all like Katy, was remembering his life up there, and the trip he later took to rediscover what had occurred.

He had a flat tire soon after he started north. The tire that went flat was new. It was supposed to be puncture proof. When the tire was taken off the rim and repaired, the man fixing it found a hand-forged nail stuck in it.

The old cut nail was from a house built before the mass production of nails changed their style, and may have fallen off a truck in front of him along the road. Maybe the truck was carrying, in sections, or pieces, an old house to be put back together.

The nail was exactly like the nail he had retrieved from the ashes of the fire that almost killed Katy. It was exactly like that nail. Of course, millions of other nails from that era looked exactly the same, but there it was, in his tire, stopping him, the same kind of nail, the only thing he had saved from the fire. Everything else had melted or burned up. Even the old cast iron cookstove had deformed, and shrunk to the floor like liquid, the same stove that had a hundred years of flames in its firebox, the same stove that had sustained all of that, melted in the house fire.

He had returned a few days after the fire, and removed the nail from the ashes. The house that burned wasn't the house in Maine. They had moved to another place, in the middle of nowhere again, and he had hidden her away there, studied her, tried to get control of her, and himself, and then the place burned.

There was the fire, and then later she almost died again, and then there was nothing. He had not seen her in years. Just the nail, which he kept in his top drawer.

Now there was this new nail, in the tire, on the way to visit the old farm in Maine. If there was ever a sign to go, or a sign not to go, the nail was it. How to interpret the sign was the problem.

The nail said, stop, you cannot go. You must not go. I will stop you if you do not stop yourself. The nail said, go on, but pause a moment, and reflect on what has been, and why you are going, and what you should be thinking.

He kept that nail, for a couple of hundred miles, then threw it away in a trash can at a rest stop. He continued on to Maine. He went up the middle of the state, and beyond Bangor, and into the vast forests owned by the paper companies and stopped in a town just north of Dover-Foxcroft, near where they had lived.

It was summer. When he left the car, the black flies found him, as if they'd been waiting for his return. They bored into his forehead and scalp like they had not eaten since he left.

After looking around the town and remembering no one, and no one recognizing him, he drove to the isolated farm where everything had been so good, and then, so bad. It was a bit like a dream because of the dizziness he felt as he rounded the curve and saw the old place, looking exactly the same.

He passed by once, and then again. He turned around at the edge of a field where potatoes and sugar beets had grown. He drove back. He pulled into the drive.

The old house was connected to the barn by an ell, or a covered and sided passage, which then turned, like an elbow, into the large barn, now empty, and then, hooked to that, another barn coming back in the same direction as the house, so that the house and its barns formed a large, wide U, a square-shaped U, into which he drove his car.

A young couple came out. Monroe and the young man and the young woman talked. He told them about when he lived there. The young man did most of the talking. The woman stayed back. In her eyes, Monroe saw she was afraid of something, or worried, and his heart nearly broke as he recognized the same look in her face as he had seen in Katy's during the time they lived there. Something was happening inside this woman, and it was disturbingly familiar.

The young man invited him in. The couple looked much like he and Katy had looked when they were up there, and even acted the same, friendly and generous, but something was amiss, evident to anyone who would spend any time with them, and evident to Monroe right away.

The man was unmistakably jealous of every move, every look, and everything his appealing and quiet young wife did or said. He watched her intently as if to determine whether something had occurred without his knowledge. He constantly looked back and forth between her and Monroe, and Monroe could see he was one of those men who mercilessly question their wives every time they return from town, or work, or were merely out of their sight for any time at all.

Where've you been? Where'd you go? Who'd you see? What'd you say? Where did you go after that? And then where? Did you go anywhere on the way from there to the next place? Did you stop anywhere? Did you stop anywhere else? What took you so long if you only went there? Did you talk to anyone on the phone? Did anyone call you? Did you see anyone in the store? Did you see anyone on the road? Who?

On and on and on and on. Some of these men and women ended up in the emergency room. He heard their stories, enough to fill in the blanks. A man did not have to take a woman up into the wilds of Maine to act out his confusion of absolute control of her. It could happen anywhere. It could happen in the middle of New York City, in a Manhattan apartment. It happened every day. All over.

This young man had it bad. He suffered from it, much like Monroe had at one time, and he was making his wife suffer from it, much like Monroe, he now knew, had done to Katy. Monroe had been dazed and confused, and jealous and mean, and had wanted Katy so much it had been impossible to have her as much as he wanted her, but now that it was over, he could see it, and what was more, he could see it in the young man, and in the look of the wife's eyes, and it made him want to tell them, both of them, things that were none of his business, made him want to help the lovely and frightened young woman, and explain to her what was happening, and why it was happening, and what it meant, and what might be in the future, and to tell the young man as well.

They walked around the farm together, saw the

fields, the upstairs of the old house which Monroe and Katy had only used for storage, but was now being used as an art studio by the new woman of the house, a sanctuary, no doubt, for the girl whose eyes revealed so much.

Later that day, though they asked him to stay the night, he began driving back south. It took two hard days to return. The whole trip, the old, defunct, isolated farm and the bits and pieces of their life up there, and now this new woman who was so much like Katy that it was positively unnerving, almost too disturbing, to think that another man had married the same kind of woman, and had found this same place, and had taken her there, and the same, the very same things, or worse, were happening, was so unnerving and confusing and sad to Monroe as he drove back down south, because he could do nothing for them.

He could have written to her. He thought about writing her. He wanted to write her. He thought about writing to them at first, and then to her. But he did not do it. He knew it would have been wrong, and the husband would have opened her mail, found her letters, questioned her mercilessly, and so he did not. It would have been right, of course, like so many other things, and wrong, at the same time.

Lydia was lost in her own thoughts while Monroe dreamed about his trip to Maine, but she came in and out of them, and looked at him numerous times, and wondered where he was, and what he was thinking. Finally, he looked at her, and smiled.

"A penny," she said, respectfully, and quietly.

"Oh, it was nothing. Just sitting here, enjoying the quiet of this place. That's all."

She admired him. She admired his education, and his quiet manner, and his way of treating her, when they got along, which was most of the time, she knew, and was so much better than the crude and hard-drinking men she had been twice married to before she met him.

She herself had been thinking about a trip. Like a married couple who awaken in the morning and find out they had the same dream, they sat beside each other, both thinking of places far away.

"What are these things?" she asked, placing her hand in his, and showing him the spots in her finger-nails that she'd always wondered about.

"These white spots?" he asked.

"Yes. I was sitting here thinking about taking a trip to the mountains, and I just realized, here I am married to a doctor, and I can . . . ,"

"Married?"

"You know what I mean, and I can finally ask him what I never remember to ask my regular doctor when I am in his office."

"Well, Lydia, I didn't want to tell you this, but since you've asked, I suppose I'll have to. Now, I don't want you to get upset, but those spots are called *punctate leukonychia*."

"They are? You mean I've got something?"

"Yes, Lydia. You do. I'm sorry."

"Well, why didn't you tell me? What do they mean is wrong with me?"

"Well, if memory serves me, they can mean anything from arsenic poisoning to leprosy."

"Oh, come on. You know I don't have any of those."

"Or, sweet girl, they could indicate typhoid fever, rheumatism, gout, myocardial infarction, or even frostbite."

"Are you making this up?"

"No. You asked, darling girl, and I'm forced to tell you. Most likely, though," he said, and held her fingers to his lips and kissed them, "it means you have defective keratinization, or maybe, my little angel, some air bubbles under your nails."

"Oh. Is that it, really?"

"That's it."

"And there's nothing to worry about?"

"Not one thing."

He kept her hand in his and continued kissing her and playfully biting her fingers, and she got chills up and down her arm where he was kissing her fingers, and she went limp and lay against him like a cube of ice that had melted all over him.

"That feels so good I can't describe it. Don't stop."

Across the road was a ravine. On either side of it were houses. The land leading into the ravine was steep, and fell away from the curb immediately. The sidewalks stopped in front of the houses on either side, and a narrow path connected them across the ravine.

The neighborhood had been constructed the way all fine houses and lots were laid out in the twenties or thirties. Wide streets and large lots and paved walks on both sides, and open spaces between the houses. There was a generosity to the setting. There had been plenty of land. It was also considered the right thing to do. The houses, with their wide sideyards and deep backyards, separated the families from each other. They were there, lined up along the street, but there was the correct distance between the houses to allow the families to live their lives in relative privacy.

The backyards, all of them a hundred feet deep or more, were the domain of the children, and the tall hedges surrounding these yards had passages through them going in different directions, similar to the one Ronnie used to visit Monroe.

The street was quiet at night. The builders of this old neighborhood, who had done the work in the 1930s, had not calculated there would be a time when Monroe and Lydia would be on their porch, and would need the space between them and the rest of the world, and would need the shelter of the oaks that had been left when the lots were cleared, or planted when the houses were built. None of this had been thought out in terms of need, but had been done because it was the right thing to do. That was all.

Now, more than fifty years later, Monroe and Lydia had this cool, empty space between them and the rest of the world, and had this quiet time before night fell, when there was enough silence and distance remaining from the plan for human life from years earlier, to contemplate and reflect on the events of their lives, of the times, a slowly rolling, languorous newsreel of the day.

"Let's go to bed early," Lydia said.

"A wonderful idea."

They took a shower. One shower. They took it together. Lydia knew this would be a night she would think about for a long time. She loved making up. She loved getting along. She loved being in love.

They turned on the TV. They watched nothing in particular, but the set was the focus that filled the pauses between the kisses and play. Monroe felt good. He wanted to make up for being cold to Lydia. It was easy to get mad at someone. It was not easy to stop. There were remedies available. The magazines were full of them. The talk shows were full of them. It was not easy to understand why it happened. It felt good when it was over. It made one want to give a lot to the other person. Making up reminded people how much of a thrill it was to please another person, and how simple it could be.

"Just name it," Monroe said. "This is your night. You can have anything you want."

"I just want you."

"You've got that, but I want this to be your night."

They got into bed.

"Let's just be close," she said. "Just hug and kiss and all that."

They did that.

"Now what?" he asked. He wanted to give her a present.

"Just anything. I love anything you do."

"I know that, but this is your night. I want you to think of something special. Just imagine you could do anything, or have anything, any way you wanted it. And then tell me."

"But I don't know. I really don't know what."

"Imagine something you've thought about, but have never done."

"Oh, gosh, Monroe, I've done everything."

"You have?"

"I don't mean that, that way. I mean, you and I just doing what we do is everything."

"This is different. This is your night, baby. I want you to have the wildest night ever, the best."

"Well, let me think, then," she said, trying to get into the same mood he was in, certainly happier to be there than fighting and sleeping alone.

"Anything," he said.

"There are some things, I guess."

"Like what?"

"I mean, some things I might have kind of thought about. Maybe."

"Just name it."

"But I can't say them. Not actually tell you."

"You can tell me anything, baby. Anything."

"Some things would be embarrassing," she said.

"No, they wouldn't. It's a game. We're playing."

"Okay, then. Well, let me think. I guess . . ."

"Whisper it, if you're too shy to say it."

He really did like her, so much. She was so much easier to be with than Katy had been. She was uncomplicated, and out in the open, and simple, and lacking in pretense of any kind.

"Well, maybe . . . ," she started to say.

Her reluctance and shyness made her all the more attractive.

"What, sugar? What is it? You can trust me. You can tell me anything."

"You'd laugh."

"I would not."

"I know you would laugh at me."

"I promise."

"You swear?"

"I swear."

"Well, if it's something I might have just thought of, or maybe read about somewhere, but not really, I mean, not really want to actually do I don't think, or whatever, but if it's just something I kind of always wondered about, then it might be . . . ," she said, and whispered it into his ear.

A car came down the street. Its muffler was loud. It sounded like Lydia's car. Monroe went over to the window.

"Where are you going?" she asked.

The car's muffler was loose. As it crested the hill and came into view, Monroe saw the muffler dragging on the pavement beneath the car. Sparks sprayed up around it. The driver lost control of the car for a moment, and bounced off the curb, and back into the road. The muffler and the tail pipe fell completely off then and lay in the shadows beyond the illumination of the streetlight, like a body, headless with only the torso, the muffler, and one skinny leg, the tail pipe, remaining.

"If that's the kind of thing you like, it does not interest me," he said, and walked out of the room.

BOB WAS ALONE. The woman was gone. The woman more stupid than the dog on the porch, was gone. It was an event to celebrate. She'd finally taken the hint. The woman was gone. The woman was gone and he was free. Some of her clothes were gone, and some of the things from the kitchen were gone, and some of the furniture was gone, but so was she, and what did anything else matter but that.

It was glorious. He could do anything he wanted. He did not have to look at her stupid face ever again. He did not have to hear her stupid conversation again. Her mindless chattering. Her absolutely and utterly, absurdly, childish ideas about everything. And she had left. She was the one who had left. Not he.

He poured a glass of milk. Just before he put it to his lips, a gray object floated to the top. The little gray thing was a silverfish, and the silverfish started swimming around, once it got to the surface.

The silverfish was a good swimmer. That must have been how it got its name. It scurried around in the milk, making ripples but going nowhere. It was as if its rudder had been left off, and it went around in a circle.

A silverfish is a horrible-looking creature to find running across your clothes when you open a drawer, or to watch scrambling up the wall and into the crack between the cabinets and the paneling, but as bad as it looked when you turned on the lights and surprised it in its act of sliming all over your house, it was nothing compared to what it looked like floating on the surface of a glass of milk. Nothing.

Bob watched it swim. He got the milk jug out of the refrigerator and peered down the spout, trying to see if any more were in there. It must have come out of the milk. He had poured it into the glass and it had come out of the spout and into the glass.

No, that was not it. Could it have dropped from his mouth? From his own mouth. Maybe there were also cockroaches. They could crawl up his throat. He could almost sense the little feelers tickling the roof of his mouth, the legs digging into his tongue. Maybe that was what had been wrong with him all long. He was full of silverfish, and now they were finally coming out.

No, that was not it. The silverfish had been inside the glass. It had fallen down the slick, sheer side of the glass and had been there when he poured the milk. Realizing this, he poured it out. Then he took another glass. He looked carefully in this glass before he poured anything into it. He blew into it to clean it further. Then he poured the milk.

The stupid woman. She could not even keep the kitchen clean. Now, things could change. He was alone. She was gone. She was living with an ex-convict, drug dealer, drug addict, and God only knew what else. He had not seen him. Maybe he was black, as well. That would be like her. She was living with an ex-convict with twenty-inch biceps and a brain the size of a goldfish, six miles across town, in a three-room apartment.

For the moment that he let himself think about it, he looked dazed, as if he'd been struck suddenly in the back, and jolted forward. He looked that lost for a second, that confused, as if the shock of what had finally happened only then became clear, as unmistakable as a silverfish in a glass of milk.

It was like, as he, uh, tried to, uh, think, uh, about it, a bit like, kind of a, well, uh, coming home, uh, one day, and uh, there's uh, well, uh, nothing there, uh, no wife, no children, ummm, no house, no street, no town, no nothing. Gone. A bit, uh, like that.

CHAPTER 12

ONROE WAS UPSTAIRS, AT the window. A light
was on in the house to his right. Ronnie's house was
to his left. He could not see her house from where he
was. Far across the ravine, through the trees, he could
see another light in another house. No driveway connected this house to their street. It must have been a
house that could be approached by car only from an
existing driveway to another house, or from a distant
road.

He opened the window. He could hear noises from
a construction site. He could hear the sound equipment made, when, in compliance with safety regula-
tions, a horn beeped when a machine was in reverse.
Somewhere, out of sight, in the middle of the night,
a yellow piece of equipment was backing up. The
horn beeped. Everyone had to clear out of the way.
Someone might be killed. Someone might be crushed.
Someone might end up on a table with Monroe staring
at him, in the same distracted way he was now looking
off into the distance. A nurse might slap him on the

back, to force him to recognize his duty to the victim.

"Why did you do that?" Lydia asked. "Don't ever do me like that again."

"Like what?" he said softly.

"Pull something like that on me."

"I hear you," he said softly, distant, relaxed.

"Was that a trick? A joke? Was it supposed to be funny?"

He shook his head.

"Is this something you've done before? To someone else? Is this something you planned?"

"No."

"I do not understand. I just don't."

"Nor I."

"If you set me up for that, I swear, I don't know what I'll do. Did you?"

"No."

"Did you plan it all along, laughing to yourself?"

"Of course not."

"I was only doing what you asked me to."

"True."

"You kept urging me on."

"Urging you on," he repeated.

"You did. It was you, not me."

"You, not me."

"Are you trying to drive me crazy? Or what?"

"I wouldn't do that."

"Why did you walk out?"

"Walk out?"

"Just answer me."

"Yassum," he said.

"You're sick, aren't you. That's what it is."

"Yassum, Miz Lydia. I'z sick, all right."

"I just give up. You live up here if you want, and

be as weirded out as you want, and I'll go on with my
life while you figure out what in the living hell you
are up to."

"Yassum."

"Do you want me to leave? Is that it?"

"Is that what you want?" he asked.

"Do you want me to find another man?"

"Is that what you need?"

"Listen, old boy. It might happen. There's only so
much old Lydia will take."

"I wonder."

The light in the house at the other side of the
ravine was out. Lydia looked across the ravine along
with him. She had not seen the light. It went out
before she saw it.

"There was a light over there," he said.

"Where?"

"Through there. It was on. Now it's off."

"What kind of light? I don't understand."

"There must be a house in there."

"So. So what? There must be thousands of houses
out there. Thousands."

"I didn't know about that one."

He was so sincere about it, she crowded the window to see what was so important.

"What about it? Why does it interest you?"

"I don't know. It was the color, possibly. It was
an unusual yellow, the way a lamp would look shining
through a window that had an old, yellowed shade
pulled down. It reminded me of something, but I don't
know what. An old house somewhere. Or that color
yellow somewhere, kind of an orange-yellow. I don't
know. It reminded me of something."

She wanted to keep him talking. Maybe he would
reveal what was really on his mind. It seemed that

if he would relax and talk to her, she might better understand how this night could have fallen from heaven to hell so quickly.

"Tell me more about it," she said. "And show me where it was."

He pointed across the night into the woods, and she knelt beside him, and tried to see what it was.

PREGNANT WOMEN

13

SATURDAY MORNING, OLD ERNEST, Arkansas's
husband, and the Cutlers' yard man, finished breakfast,
while Arkansas herself got ready to work in the vegetable garden, to take advantage of the cool of the
morning, to chop weeds.

Before she went out, she washed up the breakfast
dishes, and talked to Ernest, who remained at the
table, taking his time, thinking, talking to his wife.

"That Ronnie's a curiosity, ain't she?" he said to
his wife, who was rinsing off the dishes before she put
them in her new dishwasher, which her children and
grandchildren had given to her on the occasion of her
fiftieth wedding anniversary.

"That whole family's a curiosity," she said.

On the wall, beside the pictures of her children
and all their children and beyond, was a plaque from
the church that honored both her and Ernest for their
lifetime of membership and service.

"I worry about that little lady," he said.

Arkansas let the water out of the sink and dried
her hands on the towel that hung on the peg Ernest

had set for her above the counter and near the window, where the sun could dry the towel after each use.

"Lots of folks worry about that little lady," she said. Ernest got up. The lawn mower and the jug of gas were in the shed behind the house, along with the garden tools, so he and Arkansas walked out together, and she got the hoe, and he wheeled out the mower.

"And the new folks next door," he said, and paused, thinking of the right way to say what he wanted to say but not be too disrespectful in case Arkansas disagreed, "well, there do seem to be something unusual about them."

"Miss Ronnie, she's crazy about those folks," his wife said. "About the man, anyway," she added, and looked at Ernest to see if she got his meaning.

"Yes, ma'am," he said, "that one of the things that worry me."

He followed her to the garden. They had owned this home and the acre of land around it for thirty years, and the soil of the garden spot had been worked so well, and enriched and nurtured so lovingly, it was as sweet and tender as the way the old couple were with one another.

"I'll be going on now," he said.

Newcomers to the South who saw old Ernest pushing his lawn mower, with the sling blade, or grass whip, tied to the handle and the jug of gasoline riding on the deck, became quiet as he passed. They stood in the yard, or at their windows, and looked at him in awe, realizing they were seeing something from long ago. They imagined the thrill of employing him, and how nice they could be to him, and how generously they'd pay him, and they wished they could hear him talk, and be a part of his kindly ways.

They felt better after he passed, and some of them swore they had heard him singing, or humming. Zip-o-de-doo-dah, zip-o-dee-ay.

Ronnie saw him, and opened the window, and whistled a bird call, a secret signal, and Ernest looked up, and smiled.

Good morning, young lady.

She was in the attic. The attic had its own door. The door closed against a permanently installed stairway, not a pulldown. The stairway was steep and narrow. At the top, the attic, with dormer windows built into the roof, opened above her like the ceiling of a cathedral. It was out one of these dormer windows that she leaned, and whistled to Ernest.

Within the divisions of the dormers, there was light. There was also one bulb that lit what was not illuminated by the dormer windows, and beyond that, in the darker, deeper recesses, were things that Ronnie found that had not been touched, or seen, or moved in years.

It was there, in a box in the dark that Ronnie had carried to the light, she found the picture of her great-great-grandmother who had lived out West and had grown up, Ronnie had learned from her father, in a house built into the ground, a house that only rose above the ground high enough to set in a few low windows and the roof. That family later moved East, and to the South.

"I could live like that," Ronnie had said. She liked the idea.

"I know you could, sweetheart," her father had said. "I know you think you could, anyway."

"I wish I lived back then," she had told him. "I wish I'd been a cowgirl, or an Indian, or something."

"I know you do, but you're better off now. Everyone is. Life was hard back then."

"Not for me, it wouldn't have been," she had said.

Ronnie watched Ernest disappear behind the house, and after he did, she climbed out the window, and sat on the sill, with her legs dangling, and brushed her hair.

After she finished brushing her hair, she ran down the two flights of stairs and out to find Ernest. He was on a ladder, leveling off the top of the hedge between the houses. He was clipping steadily and quietly with shears that looked like enormous scissors, the same way he'd cut this hedge for most of his life.

"I'm fixing to head out West," she said.

"You are?"

"I sure am. I'm sick of things around here. I'm heading West. I'm going to find me a cowboy and fall in love and build my own house and have a bunch of babies and go wild and crazy every now and again and leave this place behind me like dust," she said.

"Wonder what your mama would have to say about that," he said.

"Nothing," Ronnie said, and then zipped between the break in the hedge and into Monroe's yard.

Ernest watched her from atop the stepladder, still clipping along steadily, and he saw her creep up to the window and peer in, and then creep around to the other side of the house and look in there as well.

The runaway sprigs and late spurts of spring growth fell away behind him as he cut, and the hedge was brought back in line, and looked good. Ronnie came in view from around the far side of the house, and Ernest saw her quietly open the screen door, and slip inside.

———

IT WAS TWO weeks, to the day, since Lydia and Monroe had sailed with Roger and Cissy; it was one week since Monroe had walked away during the intimate conversation. Time passes. Things change. Every day there's something new. It was best to forgive. It was best to forget.

"Let's go swimming later today. How about that?"

Just as she asked that, they both noticed something, out of the corner of their eyes, and turned to see Ronnie, who had been standing in the doorway, back out and run off.

"That scared the hell out of me," Lydia said. "She's spooky."

"She does that sometimes."

"What?"

"Appears like that."

"When?"

"I don't know," he said. "She did it the other day."

"I don't like that."

Monroe went upstairs. He returned to his book on the Sargasso Sea. Lydia paced around downstairs. She looked out the window toward Ronnie's house. She went in the backyard and then swept the front walk, and the driveway, and then the porch.

"Are you ready to go?" she asked, sometime later.

"Sure."

"Let's try the old rock quarry."

THE UNITS IN the apartment complex where Martha and Earl lived were small. The rooms within these units were themselves small, but if love was in the air, one room was enough.

Just past noon, Earl and Selby, who had spent the night, were watching cartoons and drinking beer.

Martha was in the shower. She had already made love with Earl earlier in the morning, after which they had both fallen back asleep. She had made love with him the night before, as well. They were making up for lost time. Both of them had been in a prison, of one kind or another, and were both now free to do whatever they wanted. Anything. Any time.

The bathroom steamed up. The cheap exhaust fan which had been installed when these units were built a few years ago, had only lasted long enough to pass inspection. The one-piece fiberglass shower stall, in which Martha now stood under the water, was pitted, and absorbed the dirt and smell of everyone who had ever taken a shower in it.

The sink, set in the artificial marble vanity top, had come loose, and a layer of oily, black mold had formed where the rim met the fake marble. The toilet itself was loose on the floor, due to having been installed in something of a hurry. The anchor bolts, which passed through the bottom of the toilet, through the wax seal, and down into the concrete floor, were actually anchored to nothing.

The architects, themselves in a hurry, had forgotten to leave a space for the toilet paper holder nearby. The toilet paper holder, then, had been installed across the room, fastened only to the drywall, and was itself about to fall onto the floor as the screws had pulled loose. Because the paper was so far away, and the toilet itself was loose on the floor, if a person were sitting on the toilet and reached for the tissue, the toilet leaned over with her, exposing the sticky, foul wax beneath it, and the discolored and loose flange that had been set into the floor.

This loose toilet meant that a smart tenant, once noticing this, would ignore the toilet paper holder and set the roll on the back of the tank above the toilet. At first, this seemed like the right thing to do. Then later it proved not to be. The roll of paper got wet from the moisture of the tank.

Sometimes, someone in a hurry, or unfamiliar with the bathroom, would leave the roll on the floor beside the toilet. This was even worse than leaving it on a damp tank. The floor, which was covered with ceramic tile, had shifted soon after the tile company and the inspectors had finished their work. As it shifted, cracks appeared between the segments of the tile. As they did, the grout which had been laid between these segments, came loose. When it came loose, it exposed the spaces between the tile, and all kinds of hair and grit fell into these cracks. The roll, then, once on the floor, would soak up this grime and hair.

The toilet itself, having been manufactured in a hurry, did not flush thoroughly. Because of this, one often had to flush, and then wait until it refilled, flush again, wait some more, and then finally try it a third time.

Inside the one-piece tub and shower unit, the shower head had corroded, and the stream of water had diminished greatly. The faucets, which still worked, had lost their escutcheons, or cover plates, and the pipes were exposed, as well as the holes going into the walls. The roaches crawled in and out of these holes, and it was best not to look closely upon entering the stall, but merely reach in and turn on the water and hope everything would be gone before you stepped in.

The curtain rod had broken loose from its anchors and now rested on the ledge of the fiberglass stall. Because of this, one had to be careful in parting the curtain or the whole thing would fall, clanging and banging, onto the floor. If the roll of toilet paper had been left on the floor, then it would get soaked, and the water that splashed out during the time the curtain was gone, but before you could get the water turned off, would run under the tub, where the caulk between it and the floor had peeled away.

The medicine cabinet that hung above the sink had rusted inside due to the moisture in the bathroom, and the mirror, once glued to the outside of the door of this cabinet, had come loose and broken long before Martha moved in. Someone else, also long before Martha, had taken some wire and hung a smaller mirror over this empty metal space, and that was what everyone used.

The entry door to this room, which led from the hall just inside the front door straight into the bathroom, no longer latched properly, due to the settling of the floor. Because the floor had sagged, the jamb which contained the keeper, or the slot where the latch should engage, was now out of line. Someone had tried to screw a slide bolt onto the door to use as a lock, but because the door was hollow, all the screws except one pulled out. The latch now swung from its one screw, but it was possible, if you lifted the door with one hand, and held the latch in place with the other, and then used one of your fingers to slide the bolt into its corresponding bracket, to actually lock the door.

Martha was not worried about locking the door. She was not worried about the toilet rocking back and forth. She was not worried about the roaches scampering in and out of the holes. She was not worried about the slow drain in the sink due to the wads of hair and phlegm and dirt rolled up in the curved trap at the bottom of the drain like something out of a nightmare. She was not worried because the sex was so good, and because she could do anything she wanted, and because she was free and alive for the first time in years.

THE ROAD TO the quarry was unpaved and full of holes. A sign in the weeds gave the hours of operation of the defunct gravel pit. The bushes and trees on either side of the road were covered with dust. The dust also boiled up from behind the car they followed, and then from behind their own.

The quarry itself was a large, sheer-sided hole in the ground. Around it was not grass and beach, but trees, scrub growth and pine. From the air it might have looked like a crater from a meteor.

"It's spooky, isn't it," she said.

There were people at the top of the cliff, and they had coolers with them, and radios the size of briefcases.

"I might swim all the way across," she said.

Cars were parked around the edge, and people were camped for the day, or longer, with tents and blankets and pickup trucks with covered beds.

"Or I might just jump off that cliff and scream," she said.

They parked. Lydia asked Monroe if he liked her bathing suit.

"It's a one-piece. I have not worn a one-piece in ages. Most people our age don't have their figures anymore. But my mother kept hers forever, and I think I will too. Don't you?"

Monroe unpacked his book and a chair and the blankets and closed the trunk. Dust splattered into the air around the lid.

"A one-piece is safer, anyway," she said. "After what happened before, you know."

They went into the water. It was cold, warm on top, but cold a few feet below the surface.

"This is the kind of lake monsters live in," she said.

RONNIE AND HER parents were in the sun room. The sun room had once been an open porch on the side of the house. It was now enclosed with glass.

Ernest had finished mowing. He was sweeping the walks and the driveway. It was Saturday afternoon. The old television set had been moved to the sun room when the new one arrived. A baseball game was on. Mr. Cutler was watching the game. Mrs. Cutler was looking at a magazine, and eating candy. Ronnie was playing with a pistol.

The pistol was part of the outfit she had assembled earlier in the day, because the night before she had watched one of her favorite Roy Rogers and Dale Evans movies on the cable channel.

The baseball game Mr. Cutler watched was unusual, because it had been announced that a woman would be playing. This was a major league contest, so it was more than unusual to see a woman step up to the plate, with a bat in her hand. This woman was, in fact, the first woman to ever play major league ball.

There was a runner on first and second. The woman went to the plate, and on the way, decided to bunt left-handed. She had been practicing her left-handed bunt in secret, with a friend, but she had never done it in any game before.

The crowd was roaring. The woman at bat could hardly hear herself think, and never even saw the ball as it came over. She moved the bat in bunting position, and connected perfectly.

Because of the noise and because of the unexpected hit, she watched the ball roll down the third
baseline, the same way it would have rolled down the
first baseline had she bunted right-handed, and then,
confused, she started off, momentarily, toward third
base, forgetting at the most crucial moment in her life
which way she was facing.

She realized her mistake and started back the other
way. It was too late, and everyone had seen it, and the
crowd, roaring a few seconds earlier, was silent. The
runner on second made it to third, and the runner on
first slid into second, but the woman was out, and her
perfect sacrifice bunt would forever be forgotten in
the memory of her running off toward third.

"She ran the wrong way," Mr. Cutler said.

Mrs. Cutler flipped through the pages and ate
another piece of chocolate. Ronnie returned. She sat
on the floor, with her knees up.

"She ran toward third," the old man said.

It was Saturday afternoon. The next-door neighbors were gone. Ernest was nearly finished. Clouds
were building up in the west, and it was looking like
rain. The creek in the ravine across the road would
fill up. It would roar in the night if the rain were
heavy. That would be nice.

"She went the wrong way," Mr. Cutler said.

"WHAT ARE YOU thinking about?" Lydia asked.

They were on a blanket, at the quarry, in the sun,
and Lydia was running her fingers up and down her
own arm, tickling herself, and giving herself goose-
bumps.

"You've just been so quiet all day."

Monroe turned on his side. Lydia, on her back,
put one of her legs over him, either to keep him from

rolling any further, or because it felt good to spread her legs and stretch like that.

"I thought we were going to have a good time this afternoon," she said. "Maybe we are. Maybe it's a matter of the state of one's mind. If you think you're having fun, then you are. Right?" she asked. "Huh?"

He was thinking about Katy, how years earlier he had come home one day and found her gone. That evening, he heard from the psychiatric wing of the hospital that she had voluntarily admitted herself, in consultation with a resident, and was now requesting he bring her some of her clothes, a book, her diary, her toothbrush, and so forth.

He was allowed in the locked ward. The nurse followed him to the room. It was a private room. It had a bed, an easy chair, a locked wire mesh window, and a bathroom.

The nurse went through the suitcase, article by article, and made certain there was nothing Katy could use to harm herself, or that Monroe might have brought with him to harm her. In these situations, one never knew.

Monroe was furious at Katy. This was the wrong response, and he knew it. This was not the way he had learned to be with someone sick, but it happened anyway. She was his wife. One might have thought a man would have not only the understanding and compassion he had for other people in trouble but more. Most of the time, this was not true.

The route to the psychiatric wing was a serpentine one. An escalator took visitors to the second floor, and then, in a far corner, was an elevator that only went to that wing. It would have been confusing for anyone from the inside to know where the actual wing itself was located in relation to the outside of the building.

Monroe was allowed one visit a week. After his first, he did not return. He was still upset with her for admitting herself the way she had, without telling him a thing about it, or warning him, or letting him consult with a colleague. Because of that, he told no one, and left her on her own. On his one visit, they had an argument. They became loud. The nurse appeared. She opened the door, and stood in the opening, reading a chart, for the remainder of the visit.

On the way to the emergency room one morning, Monroe noticed a few people casually looking at something. He looked as well. There was someone standing in a window. The windows were large. They were six feet tall. This person was standing on the ledge, inside the room, inside the window, with her arms above her head, holding on to something at the top of the window to brace herself in the frame so she would not fall backwards into the room.

It was Katy. The psychiatric wing was directly over the trauma center, but six floors up. At first, he did not know it was her. Then he did. He stopped, and covered his mouth with his hands until he saw her smile, and wave.

She had discovered, days earlier, that she could see him arriving at work from her window. He never looked up. Finally she thought to stand in the window so he would notice her. This was the first morning she had tried it, and it had worked. She waved. He did not wave back. After he realized she was safe and only getting his attention, he continued on.

He never looked up again. She was there every morning, and he never looked up again. He could see the other people when they noticed, and some always did, but he walked past them, and never looked up again.

That time he did look up, and saw her framed in the window, was the last time he ever saw her. She was discharged three weeks later, and went to live with her parents and then to the mountains.

"I've got a cramp, or something, in my foot," Lydia said. "In the arch."

He sat up. Lydia's leg slid into his lap, and he caught her foot in his hand and looked at it.

When a doctor examines feet, he looks for signs of swelling or discoloration. Discoloration could indicate bruising or hemorrhage. If the complaint is centered in the area of the arch, it could be a condition known as astragalus, which occurs most often in women, and is a result of rigidity of the tissues, and the spasms of the muscles' efforts to overcome the rigidity.

"That feels better," she said after he rubbed it.

Monroe read. The woman in the Sargasso Sea was improving. She did not remember what had happened. The trauma to her head had affected her brain's ability to convert what had happened into permanent memory. Neurologically, she had been given a gift, and spared the horror of her accident.

As she regained her health, the man helped her any way he could. He held her, and rubbed her swollen face, and gave her encouragement and solace, and she began to understand where she was, and that she would be cared for, and would be safe.

Time passed. There was no rescue. The man discovered the woman could not speak English. Maybe the blow to her head had knocked out all the words she had ever known.

Later, during recovery, her legs failed to function properly. She could not walk without his help. When they made love, she lay still. They began to make a life. The life they made in the vortex of the Sargasso

Sea was a good life, away from the confusion and corruption of the rest of the world.

The man told her about the ships he had discovered, and how, at the very center he thought, would be the first ship that ever sailed the North Atlantic and did not arrive at its destination, and did not sink, but lost its crew and became adrift, the first ship in history to become stranded in the mass of the Sargasso weed, and in its currents, and as he told her all this, she smiled, and understood, and accepted what he told her.

"Have you finally finished that book?" Lydia asked.

He handed it to her.

"I tried to read it already," she said. "The other day, I picked it up to see what it was all about, but I couldn't connect."

He took it back.

"I can't read when I'm distracted. I can't concentrate."

He put the book on the blanket, and lay against it. The sun had warmed the cover, and the cover warmed his cheek.

"I either read the same paragraph over and over, or the whole page goes into a blur."

A couple jumped off the cliff. They held hands. The man fell faster than the woman and had to let her go. It was thought that objects, no matter their weight, fell at the same speed. This was not true. Women had long ago evolved from birds, and some of them could still fly. Men evolved from land animals, and dropped like rocks once they left the earth.

"I like to read, though. I should have did it more when I was in high school, I guess. It seems like a good thing to do. To learn about things, you know."

A group of children floated on inner tubes from car tires. The tubes were lashed together into a crude raft.

"That's dangerous. My daddy would never let us play in the water on car tires like that."

"Tubes," he said.

"Gosh. Oh my, goodness gracious. You can talk."

He rolled up his blanket and opened the trunk.

"Are we leaving?" she asked. "Or are you leaving, and I'm to stay here? Or what?"

"I realized, when I saw the tubes, about your tires. How badly you need new tires. Let's get them."

"You don't have to do that."

"Yes, I do," he said.

"What do you mean, yes you do?" she asked him, as they drove to the tire store. "What does that mean?"

He shook his head, and pointed to the road meaning, don't talk, keep your eyes on the road, just drive.

"I can buy my own tires, I'm sure. I will, you know, when they get a little worse."

The tire dealership was in an old service station. The section of the building with the plate glass windows was still there, but additional bays had been added beside the two original ones. Stacks of tires lined the walkway in front of the building. The tires were on their sides, flat, about waist high, the height and depth of a barrel.

"I might sell this old car soon, anyway."

A man was standing beside one of the stacks. He was eating crackers. He held the pack in one hand, and a Pepsi in his other hand. When he finished the crackers, he dropped the wrapper into the middle of the tires, and then set the can on the edge of the top tire, and walked away.

"I guess you can buy me some, if you really want to."

After the man walked away, the can tipped over, and spilled into the center of the stack of tires, and then rolled down into the bottom along with the wrapper.

"I won't want whitewalls, though," she said. "They're too hard to keep clean."

A salesman with a clipboard came out. He approached the driver's side, saw it was a woman, and went to Monroe. He and Monroe talked, and then Lydia got out, and the salesman drove the car to a spot, and set a magnetized plastic number on top.

"I don't need radials, either. Any kind will do."

They walked from the middle of the parking lot to the front of the building. Monroe leaned against a wall, and Lydia sat on one of the tire stacks.

"I don't like those kind with the big letters on them, either. You know, the kind that say, ROAD BOSS, or something."

To keep balanced, Lydia had to lean forward while her legs dangled. It was like sitting on a huge toilet seat.

"Gosh, I just had this vision," she said, and laughed, "of my car coming out of there with those bigfoot tires on it, you know, about as tall as a house. You didn't get me those, did you?" she said, still laughing.

"Shut up," he said.

"What?"

Still standing beside her, he grabbed her shoulder, and shoved her down into the center of the tires. He shoved her so hard, she went all the way down. She folded up in half, and went all the way in, so that only her face and her hands and feet were visible. She looked like a woman in a saw-me-in-half magic act, peering out while she waited to be cut in two.

Monroe walked away. She could not see him. All she could see was the ceiling above. He walked across the parking lot, and across the street, and around the corner.

LYDIA PREPARED A BIG lunch when she returned. Then she called her mother.

"We just got back from the quarry. That's why I didn't call earlier. I'm sorry I forgot to tell you we were going, but it was a spur-of-the-moment thing. I'm kind of tired now, so I don't want to talk long, and I need a nap before I can even think whether or not I can come see you tomorrow, okay? I just can't think right now. I'm just worn out. All that swimming, and then we went and got some new tires for my car, and the place was real dirty, and I've got black stuff, like soot, all over my clothes and hands, and I just need to take a shower and a nap, and then I'll call you back and we can decide. Okay? No. I'm not sure if Monroe will come with me tomorrow, or not. I'll have to see. But we'll talk later. I've got to hang up now, okay Mother? Bye."

Beside the telephone, on the table, on top of the directory, was a receipt from a taxi meter, which meant Monroe was home, and was probably there at that moment, though he had not come in to see her, and she had not noticed him downstairs. She read the receipt, and then threw it away.

She pushed her plate and her empty glass into the middle of the dining room table, and made a list on a clean sheet of paper. The list had a column labeled THEN. It had another column labeled NOW. She filled in the columns. She studied what she'd written.

She went upstairs. She saw Monroe was asleep in the chair by the window. Three opened cans of beer were on the inside sills beside him. She did not wake him. She sat across from him, the way Ronnie had, earlier in the spring.

"I know you're there," he finally said, with his eyes still closed.

"I know you know."

"There's a check on your dresser for the amount."

"I don't want it."

"It's there, anyway."

"Listen, Monroe we've got to talk."

"Uh-huh," he said, and nodded, but still kept his eyes closed, as if he couldn't wake up.

"I need to explain things to you, and you might do a little explaining to me, as well. I could be mad right now. Real mad. I could have stormed up the stairs and knocked you out that window. I could have done that. I probably should have done that. But I decided I wouldn't. I decided something else was needed, even more drastic, and though it makes me sad to think about it, and it will make me even sadder to go through with it, I think it will be the right thing. But first, we'll talk about some other things, and we'll try to get some of that understanding people are always raving about these days, and then I'll tell you what I want to do.

"See, one time, on Christmas, when my daddy still

lived with us, I went into the living room real early and he was there on the couch. I thought he was waiting for me, and I got under the covers with him, and we snuggled up, and talked about everything, and I fell asleep again, and I don't know how long I slept, but he never moved. The whole time, he never moved. When I woke up, it was light, and he was still there, in the same position, with his arm around me, and we played a little joke on everyone else, and made a lot of noise and slammed doors and stuff like that, until they all came running in, and then we opened the presents.

"See, I thought he'd been waiting for me, and that he'd done this special thing of sleeping in there, just for me. Just to surprise me in the morning, but of course, he'd actually had another fight with Mom, and that's why he was there. I didn't know it until later, when I figured it out, and I guess that's what's wonderful about being a child, because you naturally put beautiful interpretations on everything, and you have no idea about the truth, I mean, the truth when it's bad, and you only figure that out much later when you have to.

"But now I can tell, unlike some people I've known, and unlike I hear and read about the way some people are, when I'm not wanted. I can now tell that. I couldn't tell that when I was a child. Now I can tell it whenever I am with anyone. Anywhere. At home. At work. My whole adult life, I could tell that, right away. You don't even have to say it. No one, I mean, had to say it. Some people have to have it knocked in their heads every day for twenty years, but not Lydia. You understand what I'm saying. Not me. I'm not like that.

"I'm not that way because I don't want to be that

way. And sometimes, you know, even the other person doesn't even know that he doesn't want you, and so because the other person doesn't know, then everything gets confused, and crazy. But I know. I guess it's possible you don't know how you've been treating me. Of course, it's hard not to remember shoving someone down into a ring of tires, and it's hard not to remember walking off and leaving them there, and not even looking back to see that I actually couldn't get out by myself, and that I had to call for someone to pull me out, and so I guess it's possible you do know you did that, but maybe you don't. Maybe you think it happened some other way. Maybe you do.

"I'm not educated, and I always hated I didn't go to college, but I see things, and I think about things, and I can figure out, usually, what is going on. And over these past few months, I've been waiting. I've been waiting for you to get right, and to come back to being the way you were before everything changed. It's almost like you got something in your head, and maybe you don't know it's in there, and you can't get it out, like a sound or something, like a noise, like your ears are ringing, and that's all you can hear, and so, while I've been waiting, I've been thinking, and I decided I would try to explain something about myself to you, and then it might help you understand why I am the way I am, because they say you've got to talk everything out, and so I'm going to try.

"See, sugar, I really like you. I do. But things have changed so much. When you and I first got together, I was down and out, and you took me in, and took care of me, except it was, if you think about and remember it honestly, working both ways at the same time. You were kind of at a low point yourself.

"And listen, I want to tell you this, in the nicest

possible way, and I don't mean anything bad by it, but I know about Katy. I mean, someone at work told me about her, and how sick she got, and how you two split up, and I know it must have been hard on you, and still must be, not seeing her ever again . . ."

"It was for the best," he said.

"But I feel for you, Monroe. I do. I really do. But that was a long time ago, and hard as it might have been, it's over. See. It's over. And then, we met. We got together, and it was good. It was so good. But you know what? From the very first I thought, is this going to work? Is it? I wanted it to. And I tried. You seemed to like everything about me at first. Everything I said, and everything I did. It was sweet. That's the word I think of when I remember how it was. And real. It was real. This stuff, this way we are now, it's not real. It's unreal. But you know, I'm not the same kind of person you are, and I know that, and I knew it then, but I thought it might work. I wanted it to, but maybe I knew it would not. I guess it was timing, or fate, or whatever, that brought us together in the first place, and damnit all, I wish it had worked. Damnit all, I wish I knew why it hasn't, and what to do, because, see, sweetheart, I think you like me. I think you actually do like me. I think, in truth, we're good together, even if we are from different worlds, and so I am saddened now to see how you've faded away from me, and how you've turned on me.

"And listen, that's not an easy thing to say. I am shaking all over inside, even though you can't see it, and wouldn't know it, but it's hard to talk like this, even for someone who talks a lot, like me. It's hard. It is. But downstairs I made a list about things, and tried to figure out why you went away from me. I couldn't figure anything out, though. Maybe it's just men. Maybe men are that way. My father was. You never know, watching your mother and your father, what is really going on. I think he was that way, though. Like you. He used to be so nice. At first he was, and then he changed.

"I remember how we'd wait for him to come home at the end of the day, from work, and I remember how we'd be so impatient for him to get home, and when he did, he would have this routine of saying hello to everyone, one by one, and then washing up, and saying something funny, like he'd been working on what to say while he washed up, and then we'd eat supper. We'd all sit there watching him like we couldn't get over him, like, *he's home, he's home*, that's the way we all felt, and we'd watch him eat, and listen to him talk, and his voice was deep, and it made me feel soft inside, and he'd eat slowly, and thoughtfully, like he was savoring every bite.

"He'd stop now and then and tell us stories about his life, or what happened in the war, or just anything, maybe something that happened during the day, and we all sat there watching him, and listening, and wishing, it would go on forever and ever. It was so wonderful. It was like what you waited for every day, to feel that good. It was.

"And then he changed. Something happened. I don't know what it was, but something changed, and he quit talking to us, and then, as you know, since I've told you before, he left. He left us. But anyway, I suppose you probably hear this kind of thing from people all the time, but it was strange, because I never knew what happened, or why he left us, and Mother never talked about it, and he was gone.

"Kind of like you did to Katy, but, I'm sorry, I

didn't mean to say that, but you see, when you just disappear like that . . ."

"I didn't just disappear," he said.

"When you just vanish, it's awful. But it wasn't the same, and I shouldn't have said it was, because he did come back. I told you, remember, how I prayed and tried to be real good, and really perfect, and thought I could make him come back, and he did. Lo and behold, he did. He came back, and I thought I'd done it. I thought I'd made him come back to us. And everyone was happy again, and it was like everything was going to be good again, and I had done it. I had made it happen.

"That's the way children think. But then he left, almost right away, and never returned. Never a visit. A phone call, sometimes, but no visits. It was awful. Really awful. But it made me think about what people are trying to do when they leave, and it made me decide, now, I mean, not back then, I'm talking about now, it made me decide what I think we ought to do, because I'm not Martha, you know, poor thing, though she's better now, and seems to have found someone who needs her, which is nice, but I'm not Martha, and you can't stuff me into a pile of tires and walk off and then pretend everything's okay."

"Somehow," he said, "although I don't expect you to believe this, I didn't mean to do that."

"Oh?"

"I did do it, but I can't explain it. I did not mean to do it. It happened, but I didn't mean for it to happen."

"Well, it's symbolic of something, see, and I know about that kind of stuff myself because I do read, when I can, and I know that when you add up all this stuff, and the way we've been, which I don't really understand, but when you add it up, it spells bad. It spells wrong."

"Right," he said. "It spells wrong."

"See, for me and you, I kind of knew, always, or at least I always worried, that it would not last. I always worried about that. I mean, I've left all the men I've ever been with. I've left them myself, as you know, but I decided this time, this was going to be it, because, strangely enough, even though we're different, in some ways, we're alike, more alike than someone might think. You are so much more educated than me, but beyond that, we are really close in a lot of ways. But I always thought, in the back of my mind, that something would go wrong, and it did."

He looked at her, and chewed on one of his fingernails. His nails were clear, unlike Lydia's. He did not usually chew on them, but he was doing it. It was soothing, and though he knew the composition of the nail, knew that it was composed of keratin, which was an albuminoid substance and contained sulfur, and cholesterin, and other minerals, and though he knew somewhere in the back of his mind, having learned it long ago, that an adult's fingernail only grows a tenth of an inch a month, and even knew that the nails on the right side of a right-handed person grew faster than the left, even though he knew all of this, and much more, he was not thinking about it, nor was he thinking about anything at all, just chewing, and staring, lost in the feel of the nail against his teeth, the sensuous imbalance of something hard, pressing against something soft.

"I guess you're not going to tell me," she said, "what it was that's happened, because, I guess, like my father, you don't even know. But it's odd, because

I was looking for it, this time, and though I was looking for it, I missed it. Suddenly, it was here."

The part of the nail on which he'd been chewing was off, now, and he mashed the sharp point that remained against his gum, again and again, making it hurt a little, but in a pleasant way.

"So I thought, I'll come up here, and tell him this, even if he just sits there, even if it's hard to do, and I will even tell him how much I like him, as a person, as a lover, as everything, and that I still do, and because I do, here is a plan.

"Let me move out for a little while. Let me give you a little space, maybe for a week or two. Or a month? A month, if that's what you need. I could disappear myself. I could be the one who vanished this time, and then I could be the one who came back, but really came back, after we both knew it was right. Okay? What do you think of that? Or," she said, when he failed to answer, "I could not vanish completely, but could just move out, and we could still see each other a little, like have a date, but still live apart. Maybe it's hard to live with someone, day after day. Maybe that's all it is. Maybe it's that simple. So, we could find out and try it. Okay? Do you want to do that?"

"Possibly," he said.

"I guess I should have known all along it would come to this. I always wondered why you fell for me like you did. I always wondered about it. I sure did like it. I did. But I wondered about it. I understood my falling for you. But I thought, at the time, what is this all about? You were quiet, and you were well-mannered, and you still are, and I had never been with anyone like that. I liked your being quiet back then.

How come I don't, now? Why did I like it then, and hate it now?"

"You tell me," he said.

"I can't. I don't know. But I wonder what a few weeks, or a few months apart, will do for us. I wonder. It could be like the girl from the wrong side of the tracks, which is me, naturally, and the fellow she falls for, except I'm not really from the wrong side of the tracks, not that way really, but damnit all, I tried. I have tried. I thought you liked, you know, me to be, well, this is hard to say, but I thought one of the things you liked best about me was the way we were, or, anyway, what you liked about me was the way I was in bed. I thought you liked that, and I kept thinking, if I am better than anyone he has ever known then he'll love me for it. Jeez, what a dope. What a fool."

"You weren't a fool," he said.

"I thought it was what you liked about me, and what you wanted. It seemed like it. But what the heck," she said. "Tell me about the plan. Do you think it might work?"

"It might."

"Then talk to me about it."

"I don't know what to say."

"Say anything. My god, man, I've just sat here and poured out my heart to you, so say something. Tell me something, how about it."

"It might work," he repeated.

"I guess that means yes. So, I've got to figure out where to go, and for how long. But damnit all, if it doesn't work, then what? I mean, if it won't work, then what am I going to do for, well, forget it," she said, and slammed her hand flat against the wall, "just forget it. But crap, I guess I might as well face I'm going to have to start all over . . . ," she began to say, and then let it go.

"Look at my hands," she said. "Have they been shaking like this the whole time?"

CHAPTER 15

THE BEER WAS FLAT. Lydia was gone. It was late. It was quiet and the room was dark and Monroe was still upstairs and the flat, warm and watery beer reminded him of English bitters.

He had his first bitters on the way to Ireland. He was crossing from Liverpool on a passenger ferry. The Irish Sea, known to be rough at times, was unusually rough that trip. The ferry bobbed up and down, endlessly.

It was his first ocean voyage. Nearly everyone on board was seasick. It was that bad. It had not affected him. He sat on a bench, leaning against the wall of a cabin within. Inside the cabin were berths. Most of the people in the berths were sick. Beside him on the bench, and like him, leaning against the wall and looking out to sea, were two women.

One of the women was pregnant. The other woman was not, but looked much like this pregnant woman in her face. They were sisters. The sister who was not pregnant kept looking at him. She looked at him, and then away, and then again. The pregnant woman gazed out to sea, and was lost in thought. She was quite pregnant, and looked about to deliver. Maybe she was concentrating on making it to land before she let it happen.

The sister sat between Monroe and the pregnant woman. Finally, the sister, after studying him for nearly an hour, spoke. She asked him about himself. He told her what she wanted to know. Then she told him about her life, and her sister's. She told him the sister had no husband. She explained how she had been led astray, and become pregnant, and the horrible predicament she was in. The sister who was pregnant was quite beautiful, with pale skin, and reddish hair, and a lovely face.

The ship tossed wildly. It seemed to everyone on board there was a chance they might not make it. It was a difficult crossing, even for the crew. Monroe heard them comment on it to one another. It was, as time passed, possible they would not make it.

The storm, being so violent, added to the shared terror, and the resulting intimacy of the crossing. Night fell while they were still at sea, and with the night, and with the closeness of the sister, and her quiet, steady conversation, and the dreamy, sad, and very pregnant woman beside her, it seemed to Monroe they were alone, not in fact, naturally, but it seemed that way, that they had been brought together and would, if luck were in their favor, survive.

As the sister talked, she unfolded a story that Monroe became a part of. Along with the story, and the fatigue of the trip, and the storm, and the absolute blackness of the night over the ocean, he became, as well, a part of this family. Somehow, without actually knowing how it happened, or why it was happening,

Monroe felt as if he were going to marry the pregnant sister.

The older sister, who was obviously taking care of this younger girl in her time of need, never brought up the subject, but the more she talked, and the more the storm raged, and the more the ship struggled, the more it seemed to Monroe that he would ask the sister to marry him, that it would be not only the right thing to do, but the only thing he could do, given the way they had come together in this pitch-black night, on a ship floating in the middle of nowhere, and, for all he knew, about to die together.

It seemed, as well, when he looked into the pregnant sister's eyes, that she was waiting for him to ask her. She was quiet, but she was listening, and her eyes went back and forth from above the rail where the night and the sea met in the same blackness, to her lap, and now and again, but not often, to Monroe, to his face, to his eyes, and deeply into them. It seemed she was waiting, quietly waiting, for him to become her husband, and a father to the child.

He remembered the way he was drawn to her, and into their lives, like an undertow pulling sand from beneath his feet and out to sea, and him along with it, the way he had actually almost said to the woman, would you marry me, but he did not clearly remember how he got away from them, before he actually said it.

Getting away was difficult sometimes, but it was always the right thing to do, he thought. He'd treated Katy badly. He knew that, but in many ways, she'd brought it on herself, in much the same way Lydia had brought this estrangement on herself. The women in his life always seemed to change once love was declared, once the marriage began, once they moved in with him. They said, I'm yours, but they didn't mean it, he thought.

Sailing across the sea with a woman seemed a nice thing. It was just you and her and the ocean, and the undulations of the ship, and the heavy desire of the engines beneath you, and the vistas of endless possibilities. Once ashore, things changed. It did seem to him they brought it on themselves, and it did seem, truly it did, to Monroe that it was best to move on and start again, to move on, until he found the one who meant it when she said, I'm yours.

SMALLER WOMEN

16

SOMETHING HAPPENS WHEN GROWN-UPS talk to children. What happens is clear when the grown-ups are your parents. Blood rushes from one to the other, as if the umbilical were still attached. You may be sitting in chairs, on the lawn, under the shade of an old tree that might have sheltered your mother when she sat near her mother, and both felt the same as you now did as you talked.

Those are rich times. They are rare times. When it works, so much can be learned, and the supplication of being alone, or being different, or being hated, or being unloved, or confused, or angry, all diminish in those times when the grown-ups talk to their children.

Some children could only dream about what might have been, what might be, and why things were the way they were, but they knew better than to ask. There was that look on their mothers' faces, that posture, the lips squeezed clean of blood, and the bleach-whitened hands that never opened, but remained clenched in tight, arthritic fists, as if in battle, a mystery to the children who awoke every day thinking that today, yes, today will be a good day.

That is the way children lived. They looked toward the window, saw the light, and leapt up, ready to discover if it would be true. There was that chance. Things felt good. There was that clarity and crispness in the air, and the smell of everything fresh. It was possible.

The children awoke. In their enthusiasm, they flew down the halls. They leapt on their parents' bed. It might have been summer. They were home from school. Father left for work, and Mother remained with them. Mother, knowing what was in her children and feeling it exactly the same in herself, made a special event of the day. She took them for walks, and picnics, and lazy hours under the trees.

There she told them what she'd been like as a child. She told them about her brothers and sisters, and what her parents had been like, and about the times she had gotten into trouble, and the things they had done to each other, and the things, she, like them, feared. She told them how she met their father, how their lives had come to be, what they were today.

In those moments, in the cool, subdued shadows, each person existed in silhouette. The children began to understand the world, and themselves, and these people who were their parents, and what it was that happened, that brought you through your life.

Sometimes, as with Lydia, the good stopped. It stopped the way a knife falls from the counter, and stabs the floor, quivering upright, and the revelation was lost, and the vision of being a part of things, a part of this family, a part of the world, disappeared.

The children were left wondering and full of questions, but with their lips sewed shut, or their tongues removed, or their ears lopped off, or their eyes pierced by needles.

Even those who had only understood their lives once or twice were better off than Ronnie, who had never spent a lazy afternoon in a lawn chair in the shade with her mother, talking of how she came to be, and what she was, and where she would go, and what she would do.

Even those left earless, like alien creatures who listened through their skin, or smelled through their fingers, or whatever odd things would compensate for what had been lost, even those children had it better than Ronnie, who had been on her own, and fighting for herself, almost since the day she was born.

In a situation like that, the life in the child, the same force that allows the just-hatched chick to live days and days without food or water while it determines where it should go and what it is supposed to do, the life of the child endures.

Ronnie had her pictures. She had her ancestors from the Great Plains who seemed to say to her, with their somber eyes dead into the lens of that ancient camera, you and I are the same. You come from me. There is a connection here that goes beyond the lunacy of the life around you.

She was like a figure in a glass ball would be, had it come loose. When shaken, and the snow filled the globe, the figure, too, floated around, looking out at the world, but not knowing where to stand, how to act, what to say.

CHAPTER 17

LYDIA WAS GONE, AND the house was quiet, and nothing moved unless Monroe moved, or unless he moved it. It was early morning. It was four-thirty. The light across the ravine was out.

Long ago, there would have been milk trucks. If you got out early enough, you, as a child, could ride with the man in these milk trucks. There were metal racks on which you could sit. The trucks were cool, and wet, and the bottles sweated and dripped, and the man driving had no doors on his truck, and he seemed to be happy. He ran from the truck, to the house, and back again, and he let you ride down the block with him, and he did seem to be happy.

Maybe it was being up that early. He was the first person to begin the day, and therefore set the tone for the day, for the world, and was like the mythical figure who traveled early, while everyone else slept and decided what kind of day it would be.

Maybe it was when the children were riding in the truck, and only then, he felt good. Maybe on the other days, he was sour, and angry, and dragged himself from the truck and past the dogs and up the steps and read the notes that sent him back down the steps and to the truck and back inside to get one more item the people had only the night before remembered.

Then again, it might not have been that, either. It could not be known, anyway, as the milkmen, in the South, at least, were gone. The milk came from the store. It came in plastic jugs. The jugs had a handle, and had been designed so that anyone with a strong wrist could pour them with one hand. Children could not do it. The children dropped the plastic jugs, and the lids, which no longer screwed on, but instead, snapped in place or laid on top of the spout like a lid with the threaded sides cut off, the lids popped into the air when the jug hit the floor, and the milk went everywhere. It went across the floor, but worse, under the base of the cabinets, and under the refrigerator, where strange molds would begin to grow.

It was not only the children who dropped the jugs of milk. An adult, any adult, on a given day, or a bad morning at four-thirty, not having slept well, might drop the milk onto the floor, and then have to swim barefoot through it, while deciding how to clean it up, and if to clean it up, or to forget it and go to work and return later, and maybe the cats, well, there were no cats, but maybe the, the something, would clean it up. The something like, a, well, a, the something like a, for instance, a woman.

A day with a gallon of milk on a dirty kitchen floor was not the best way to begin. A day without a woman, who might, might, that is, the possibility was always there, rush in, and with soothing tones, correct the awful situation, so that you watched this goddess of domesticity in action with your mouth open and your hands at your sides, like a dumb ape who did not know what next to do, a day without any possibility that anyone but you, and only you, would soak up the milk, well, that was certainly a poor way to begin.

But one did forge on. At six in the morning, one did have to begin the duties for which one was trained, and paid, and paid well.

It was the weekend, and that made a difference. The crazy people, and the ones who were thought sane but had suddenly gone too far, came into the emergency room at all hours. Some of them had succumbed during the night, and their troubles were so immediate there was no ignoring them. In they came. Others slept through it, or tried to, and sometimes, just as Monroe was arriving so were a string of patients who had tried to cure themselves, or sleep it off, but failed.

It was difficult to live with pain throughout a long night, and through the endless, early-morning hours. A man or woman with a kidney stone might somehow make it through the day. But into the night, and then into the morning, the pain always, it seemed, got worse. It moved into that hyperventilating state of uncontrollability, and the people ended up rolling on the floor, crawling on their knees, whimpering like wounded animals and panting and gasping and baying for relief.

Ileitis could be a lot of fun. The ileum is the third part of the small intestine. The food entered at the top, or the duodenum, proceeded to the jejunum, and then to the ileum, which sometimes became blocked, caused terrible pain, and, in the old days, the cause of the blockage often turned out to be roundworms, massed together as tight as a ball. There was a strange thrill to opening someone up and discovering the worms.

THIS MORNING, THOUGH, it was worse than stones, worse than worms. Monroe sensed it, before he was told. When he was in the dressing room another doctor, going off duty, confirmed what he had thought.

"It's bad."

"I thought so," Monroe said.

"It's the kits. Those kits. They've just been stocked in all the stores."

"I heard about it last week."

"I had a man a few hours ago, came in, his penis was the size of a punching bag, and just before I could get to him, the thing exploded all over the place."

"A mess, huh?" Monroe said, getting on his white jacket.

"Mess? I don't want to think about it. They're yours now. We've got three men and eight women in there, all with the same thing."

The home enlargement kits had been distributed and put on the shelves in the past few weeks. What made it worse were the talk shows. The talk shows had spread the word, and it had been hell in the trauma centers ever since.

The kits, themselves, though cheap and shoddy, could have worked. The people should have followed the directions. The desire to enlarge had always been there, along with a few, successful anecdotal incidents.

The kits, then, on the shelves everywhere, had disposable syringes full of collagen, which was what the reconstructive surgeons used. It was an acceptable agent. In the hands of amateurs, however, it was a disaster.

The kits were legal. Evidently, if you only did it to yourself, it was legal. There were no laws on the books to stop you from doing anything you wanted to yourself. This was a fact. It was from old common law, and beyond that, was one of the tenets of capitalism.

The problem with the kits was twofold, as Monroe perceived it. One was the lag time in the reaction to the injection, and the other was there was no limit to how many kits could be bought. Many people were in such a rush to enlarge, they failed to read the instructions. They injected the catalytic agent, and then, when nothing immediately happened, they injected more until it began to show.

By then it was too late. The lag time caught up with them, and in they came. Like the man with the exploding penis, the women were also arriving. Some of them staggered in with sixty-five-pound breasts the size of prize-winning watermelons, and still growing.

"They are all yours, now, old fellow," the doctor on his way out, said. "Try to draw the fluid out as fast as you can. If you see the thing is going to blow, have a plastic sheet ready, and get the aides to cover them up and tie them down, and get the hell away. That's all you can do."

"I'll remember that."

"He blew up something terrible," he said, about to close the door. "Funny, though. The look on his face, just before he went. It seemed as if he were enjoying it. Kind of a dazed smile."

Monroe remained on the couch. He looked at the clock. It was four minutes past six. He was four minutes late. The clock was large, and round, and the numbers were black against the white background. The clock was controlled by a central computer. When it got off, it knew how to correct itself. Sometimes, unexpectedly, one of the hands would suddenly jump into a new position.

Watching the clock that morning, as he lay with his head resting on the back of the couch, the long hand suddenly did that, jumped like that, and when it did, he jumped too. At the same time, there was the muffled sound of an explosion down the hall. After the explosion, he could hear people's voices, and then footsteps as someone ran toward his room.

A nurse leaned in. She looked him directly, and sternly, in the eye, and nodded her head back toward the hall. He looked in that direction. A fluorescent light, six long, double fixtures from where he sat, flickered and bubbled along the length of its tubes. One of the tubes, while he looked, suddenly went black.

The nurse cleared her throat. She motioned with her thumb and her head for him to get moving, and get to work. He looked at the clock. It was eight minutes after six. The nurse closed the door. He followed her down the hall.

EARL AND HIS former cellmate, Selby, who was now out of prison and temporarily living with Earl and Martha, were building a bookcase. The bookcase was for Martha. Martha had a lot of books.

"You see, Selby, boy, if you read as much as we do, you'd know more about life, and you'd understand things better."

Selby held the one-by-ten to the line, while Earl nailed it through the upright one-by-ten which would serve as the sides to the bookcase.

"You can either learn by screwing up, or learn from reading about other people's screwing up."

Earl nailed the boards together with eight penny-framing nails. A good carpenter would know he'd done it wrong, and that he should have dadoed out a slot for the shelf, and then glued it, and then nailed it with finish nails, setting the heads within the wood and filling the holes afterward.

"One thing you will learn to understand, one way or the other, is about women."

The framing nails would hold fine. They would hold better than the finish nails, but the heads would show, and eventually they would rust, even indoors, and show through the paint.

"Women, you see, was created by God, but He created man first."

Another mistake Earl had made in laying out the bookcase was the span. He had bought the shelves six feet long. Even under their own weight, with nothing on them, they would sag over time.

"And the reason He did that, was because man was put on this earth to care for woman, and that's where things is got off these days."

With a load of books on the six-foot span, the shelves wouldn't last long, and they would gradually bend downward until the shelf above rested on the top of the books on the shelf below, all of them eventually supported by the books on the very bottom.

"Women has forgot how much they need men in their lives, and things just ain't natural anymore."

By the time the shelves sagged that far, you wouldn't be able to get the books out, except along the edges where the nails held the boards stiff in place.

"Once you learn how to treat a woman right, then, you see, Selby, you'll be able to get a good woman to love you, for the first time in your life, maybe."

The span was wrong, the nails were wrong, there were no diagonals to hold the squareness true, but

Earl admired Martha, and she would love his surprise, and that was what mattered.

"I'll tell you something about women, Selby. They think they can do without men nowadays. But they can't. A woman, if she don't have a man in a certain length of time, gets sick. She begins to fail, and her longing for a man makes her sick. And that's all women, Selby. Every one of them."

Besides the span, the nails, and no diagonals, Earl had used white pine, which was soft and easy to work with, but was a feast for termites and beetles, who would call their friends to share in it.

"You need to learn to treat women well, Selby. And you need to understand their sesual needs. Some of them have powerful needs. At times, you might find yourself with one what needs more than one man can offer. In that case, you do the right thing, and supply them with what they need. It's just the way life is, Selby. Once a woman gives in to her sexuality, it's likely going to take more than one man to satisfy her. It surely is."

TWELVE HOURS LATER, without a break, Monroe left the emergency room. There was a car in front of him. The car was going slowly. It was an old car and accelerated badly, and blue smoke came from the tail pipe in a weak spiral.

There was a woman driving the car. Monroe could see part of her face reflected in her outside, rearview mirror. She had dark skin. Her hair was dark, and her eyes were dark. She was alone. At a stoplight, she spotted Monroe, looking at her, and he was surprised she could tell he was watching her.

They were traveling the same direction. Then the woman turned into a parking lot at a discount store.

She bumped hard from the road into the lot, and when she did, she glanced in her mirror to see if Monroe had seen the jolt, or seen her pull in, or was turning in as well.

He did follow her. He had not intended to, but did. She parked beside a long line of cars. Monroe stopped further out. She remained in her car longer than most people do, once they've parked. She brushed her hair. The brush moved smoothly until one spot. Every time she came to this place, it snagged, and she held the hair above the brush while she pulled it through. She did this again, and again. Soon her hair lifted out from her scalp as if by static electricity, and she gathered it up in one hand and fluffed it over the sides of her face.

After that, she held the brush out the window, and pulled the loose hairs from it, and let them fall onto the pavement. Some of the hairs were caught by the breeze, and blew away.

Quite suddenly, the woman turned, and looked over the back of her seat, and through the rear window at Monroe. It seemed to him she spoke, and made a gesture, as if illustrating what she had said, but he could not discern what it had been.

She opened her door, and quickly turned toward him again, and at the same time, the breeze that had carried the loose hair away, picked up what she'd fluffed over her face even further, so that instead of being able to hide behind her hair, she was exposed.

One side of her face was gone. Completely gone. Her nose was there, but her cheek on that side, her jaw, part of her ear, the flesh down to her neck, were missing. From that side she looked like a monster. Whatever had happened to her, a tumor belatedly diagnosed, or crudely removed, or an accident that

had been handled the best it could in whatever circumstances there had been, and then left that way,
without follow-up, or repair, whatever it had been,
was horrible enough to cause Monroe, who had seen
everything, to drop his eyes, if only for a moment, and
when he did, she pulled her hair back over her face,
and put on a scarf, and walked away.

Soon it began to rain. The parking lot filled with
cars. The rain steamed on the pavement. The more it
rained, the faster people ran to and from the store.
When the woman with half a face returned, she would
have to run as well, or wait inside for the rain to stop,
or for someone to take pity on her and help her.

Sometimes, as Monroe watched, the people driving the cars pulled to the entrance, and let the family
out. Most of the time the men drove. Occasionally,
the women were driving, and sullen men were in the
passenger seat. Sometimes a woman drove up alone.
Why would a woman be alone? What did it mean?
Did it mean she wanted to be alone? Did it mean she
was alone because she could not be with other people?
Did it mean she was strong? Weak? Had failed?

It seemed all right for a man to be alone. It did
not seem the same when it was a woman. A man, out
to take the fresh air, and the exhilaration of a jog
around the block, or through the park, seemed to be
doing the right thing, as the muscles flexed, and the
blood flowed and the heart raced, but a woman, doing the same thing, alone, appeared to be out of
place. It upset some people. It made them want to
stop her.

Soon the woman with half a face left the store.
She proceeded through the rain as if she did not care,
in defiance. In one hand she had a plastic bag. The bag
had handles formed into it as part of its shape. The

bag was made of clear plastic, and Monroe could see what she had bought.

Stacked one on the other, were two boxes of Kleenex. They were not the brand known as Kleenex, but were the house brand. These house-brand boxes could be a problem. A person reaching for a blow, or a sneeze, or from a good long cry, would have to claw at the pile to get one up. Sometimes, that failed. Then the person with the blow, or the drip, or the sneeze, or the cry, would have to hold the box upside down, and shake it until one tissue separated from the rest and became available.

The woman put the bag beside her on the seat. No one else was sitting there, so it was a good place. She started the car. She drove toward Monroe. It was a shame a woman in her condition, and all alone, had to drive such a beat-up car.

RONNIE SPED OUT the front door with her mother behind her. She cleared the hedge, but her mother fell into it, unable to jump it, and unable to stop.

Someday I'll run out the door and never come back, and I'll go far away. So far away.

She thought this while she sat on the curb near the end of her street watching the water run down the gutters, across her bare feet, and up to her ankles. The rain was cool as it fell, but warm flowing in the street.

A car turned toward her, and she saw it was Monroe. She remained at the curb with a stick in her hand, catching debris as it flowed by.

"Do you want a ride somewhere?" he asked.

"No. I'm just dreaming."

"I'm beat," he said. "I need a rest. Do you want to come over later?"

"Sure. I'll be there. Sometime. I can't say when. But in a while."

"Anytime's all right."

"Later, then. I will see you later. There's someone on your porch, by the way."

"I FOUND AN APARTMENT to rent," Lydia told Martha, "and I think I'll take it right away."

"Where is it?" Martha asked.

"It's on Sunset, in that new complex. It's really nice. At first, I thought, well, better stay here with Martha, because, you never know, Monroe and me might get back together, and then like, the day I signed the lease, or something, we'd talk, and things would be like they used to be, and then I'd be stuck with that lease, but then I thought, good Lord, Lydia, you can't make your decisions based on a man, not anymore. Not these days.

"I used to, but I don't want to anymore. It's not working out. It feels good to give yourself over, but then something always goes wrong, so I went ahead and took it. The apartment, I mean. But God knows, I hate moving. I really do.

"There's something about moving that always feels to me, anyway, like the end of something, rather than the beginning. I guess that says a lot about me. Maybe this time I can make myself believe it's the beginning of something."

"It probably is," Martha said.

"Yeah, but what? How can something be the beginning of something when you don't know what
you're starting? Anyway, I'm working on it, believing
in this move as something new and good, and even if
we do get back together, it will have to be in a new
way. I think it will. I mean, in the way it was in the
beginning, but different. Oh hell, I don't know what
I'm talking about."

"I understand what you mean."

"I know you do. But moving, good Lord, I hate it
even if it does mean something good. Moving furniture
and all that. Which means I'll have to see Monroe
again and move out what little I have there, but I guess
it'll be a good time to talk, and to quit playing games.
I hate playing games. I'm too old to play games. That's
why, just before I left, I told Monroe all about my life,
and told him the things I thought would make him
understand me, and understand us, but it didn't work.

"It's awful to start over. It's awful to love a man
as much as I do, and have so much trouble with him.
I don't know what it is. I get lonely, and then I meet
someone, and I see all these things that aren't really
there."

"We all do that," Martha said.

"I guess I may as well face I might lose Monroe,
but then, really, so what? Right. There's millions of
them out there, although, he is a good man in many
ways. And so much a better man than I've ever had
in my life, even with his faults. He might change,
though. He might even be changing right now, thinking about things, and realizing things, and all that.

"I hate it when I get like this, and get that feeling
of utter, hopeless loneliness, and the feeling of having
nothing, and not going to have anything. No more fun,

no more sex, no more nothing. Oh, I know I'll live, but I just hate it when I have to start all over again with another man. Really. I hate it. And always, after a while, after a long time of not having any sex, or affection, or whatever damn word you want to use for it, I get weird feeling, self-conscious, or whatever."

"How does not having affection make you feel self-conscious?" Martha asked.

"I don't know. I don't know what I'm saying. I guess I'm trying to face the fact that Monroe probably won't want me back. And that I'll have to start all over again with another man, and that's always such a waste, after you've got everything worked out with one, you have to start all over again with another one.

"And what if Mother calls, and finds out I'm gone. Then I'll have to hear one of those I-told-you-so sermons. I know I have to tell her, sooner or later, but I hope it's later, and I'll have something else good, I don't know about what, but something, to tell her at the same time."

AFTER BELATEDLY HEARING that Lydia had temporarily moved in with Martha and Earl, Bob decided to visit Monroe, and do a little drinking, and have a grand old bachelor night of it, and it was he who Ronnie had seen on the porch, and who now waved his hand in greeting as Monroe drove up.

"The bitch couldn't do anything. She couldn't even run," Bob said, already high from the gin he'd brought with the beer.

"Couldn't run?" Monroe asked, wishing he weren't there and had the nerve to back out the driveway when he saw who it was.

"She could not even run. Not even across the yard. I saw her try once, and I thought, the damn fool woman cannot even run. She can't cook, she can't screw, she can't think, she can't do anything."

"It wasn't that bad, was it?"

"We'd gotten a couple of chickens one time," Bob said, "because she had to have some chickens. Hens, I mean. We'd bought these three acres, which cost practically nothing at the time, but's worth a fortune now, and old Martha, bless her fat soul, had to have some hens. So we got some, and sure enough, as soon as they were old enough to fly, they began flying over the fence."

"How high was the fence?" Monroe asked.

"I don't know how high the damn thing was, but it was hell to get them back in. Have you ever tried to catch a chicken? They've got these tiny legs and no brains, absolutely no brains, they were the only things I ever knew dumber than Martha, but they can run like the wind and turn on a dime and it's hard as hell to catch them. You have to run them into a bush or run them into their own fence, which you can do, and they run straight into it and get their heads caught in the mesh, but that's not the point. The point is, I refused to chase them after a while, and Martha had to do it, along with the boys."

"Your sons probably liked it."

"For a while, but the point is, do you know, I had never seen her run before I saw her chasing the hens. Think of it. How many times in your life have you actually seen your wife run? How many times in a man's life does his wife actually run anywhere? Until recently, I suppose, with all the jogging and so forth, but that poor old gal was trying to catch the chickens and she did not know how to move her legs. She bobbled up and down, and I could have died laughing."

I wish you had, Monroe thought. Or would go on and die now, and let me get some peace and quiet and rest.

"I saw her out there, and I had that sickening feeling, that sickening revelation that this was what I'd married. Why does a man marry such a woman? I ask you. Why? She could do nothing. Nothing. She just lay there and did nothing."

"She's all right," Monroe said.

"I don't know what the trouble was between you and Lydia, but at least Lydia's a peach, a real peach. I should have done better for myself. I don't even know why I married her. She was just there, at a certain time, and then, there it was. A lifetime of hell for a few nights in bed. Isn't that just the story of a man's life?"

"For some."

"I ought to write that. I bet men would like to know it happens to other men. You observe how, these days, women get all the press about everything. The man's always the villain. I tell you, it works both ways."

"It works both ways," Monroe said.

"They push you and push you, and one day you punch her, and bam, you're in court, you're in the papers, and your career is over. You're a dead man. It could happen to anyone. Haven't you ever been mad enough to hit a woman?"

Years ago a house burned. Katy was Monroe's wife at the time. It must have been their house that burned.

Various things were lost. Some of what was lost could be cataloged. Some could not. Monroe lost Katy, and she lost him. They had been lost to each other for a long time, but the fire illuminated the loss. It made it real.

No one really knows how fires start. Experts claim to know, but they don't. What went on in the hearts and minds of the people in the houses, the words spoken, and even worse, those unspoken, were the true reasons for fires.

If one wanted to start a fire in an old farmhouse, it would be easy. One would pour kerosene on the floor, light it, and run. The floor itself, and the walls, and the framing behind them, were full of turpentine. The old pine lumber used years ago to build these houses was full of pitch, and that was why they stood so long.

Termites could not eat that wood. Water could

not penetrate. Tight grained, and full of dark poison, it lasted. Fire, though, loved this wood. These houses burned like hell itself once aflame. They burned with deep yellow and orange, exquisitely beautiful flames, terrifying, and unforgiving.

When a house fire began inside, the interior surface of the dwelling could often be fully ablaze before it breached. If a man or woman were to come upon a house on fire, and all the fire was still inside, and the windows and doors were closed, and that man or woman opened the door, the flames would suck in the oxygen, and, at the same time, drag whoever opened the door into the fire. It was best not to open the door of a house on fire.

Sometimes, though, you would have to open the door. Your wife might be inside. Katy might be inside. The fire department might not have been called. No one had seen the flames but you, as you drove up coming home from work. Then, in that situation, you must go in. Your hand must grasp the knob, even if it is hot.

At times, in the life you might have shared with this woman, you may have wished her dead. Now was the moment to make good on it. If you meant it, when you thought it, when you said it, why not walk away?

If a woman, a young woman, a lovely young woman were standing in a room full of flames, the first thing that would go would be her clothes, or her hair. She would look marvelous for a few seconds, so radiant, and aglow.

Sometimes, when a woman wanted to look hot, and passionate, and alive, she made her hair seem fiery and loose and ablaze with light. That was what a woman who had just that second caught fire would look like. But only for that one, single second.

Then, the hair would burn off, and she would begin to look like a concentration camp woman, and the skin would melt, and the inhuman sounds would come out of what was left of the lips, and then nothing would come out, because the lungs would be scorched and full of smoke.

If the house was far away from town, the rural fire department would be called. These trucks would carry their own portable tanks. They would set them up rapidly. A pond would be located. A relay of trucks would make run after run. The tank would be filled, and the pumper truck would draw from it and onto the flames.

Is there anyone inside?

This was the first question the fire fighters asked. Here was another one of those moments. No. You could say no. You could say, I'm not sure. I don't think so. There's not supposed to be. You could say, I don't know. Or, you could say yes.

Those questions would not have to be asked if you had already gone in after your wife, and pulled her, dragged her, led her, or asked her to follow you, please, out the door to safety. Then the fire fighters might only ask, is there anyone else inside.

What did they mean by anyone else? Anyone's soul? Anyone's spirit? Anyone's life, burning and melting away from years and years of smolder?

Of course, they only meant, are there other people inside.

People in accidents often reported that what occurred seemed to be in slow motion, or was happening to someone else. The person pulling the trigger and plugging seven holes into another person, sometimes said it was like someone else doing the shooting. I heard the shots. It was like they were coming from somewhere else.

Imagine spending a whole night in that state of mind, where everything seemed to be happening to someone else, or to this person beside you, who looked like you, but was not. Many people have reported those times in their lives.

Imagine spending years like that. It was like, she said, I don't know how to say it. It was like, it was not happening to me. It was like, all of this, everything he did to me, everything that went wrong was happening to someone else. I was there, and I could see what was happening, but it was as if it were another person.

Some people got that way. They had to. It was all they had left, to detach and let life, the life as they had come to know it, happen to this other person and not to them.

A long time ago, before the fire, before the hospital, a young man, a young medical student, met a woman who glowed from the joy of being alive. Seductive and passionate, she flew against him like a child, seeing something in him that needed her in a way she'd never been needed before. She wrapped her legs around his waist, and cried from the sweetness of it all.

It felt good. At first, it felt so good. The need was so great, and nothing had ever quite felt so good, so intense, before. It was a sensuous encumbrance, like walking through water. The water was waist deep. The legs moved slowly. The smile was fixed, on the face. The hands trailed behind, floating on top of the water. The body swayed, a pendulum of deep and heavy desire.

MARTHA PAINTED HER TOENAILS red, which was the same color Lydia had done hers the night before, in her own apartment, while they talked on the phone. Martha had not painted her toenails in years.

"I was reading an article this morning, before I came over," Lydia said, "and it was about a time when all the men were gone, during the siege of Leningrad, and I got interested in it because it made me wonder what it would be like to live that way, with no men because there were no men around, not because there were no good men, or whatever, but just because there were no men, and I decided it was all just a state of mind, and because of that I've been working on myself to accept being alone, and not worry about it."

"Everything's a state of mind," Martha said, as she bent over her big toe with her mouth open and her tongue out, concentrating.

"Yeah, I guess it is," Lydia said and uncrossed her leg, and squeezed her foot to get the blood circulating again.

"You make your own state of mind. That's what's awful about it," Martha said. "I thought I loved Bob. I didn't. I never did. I was too young when I married him. Because things didn't work out the way I thought they would, I began to pretend and to lie. I pretended and I lied for 23 years."

"I've been there myself," Lydia said.

"I lied because I didn't want to face what I'd done, and admit what a jerk I'd picked to marry."

"Amen."

"I let him run over me. If you marry a good man, and are nice to them, they love you for it. If you marry a Bob, and you're nice, they run over you and take you for all you're worth."

"Yep. I do know what you mean."

"You know, Bob bought his first BMW when he wasn't making a penny. He had no job, and he'd just finished grad school, and he went out and bought it, and came home whining and crying to me about how he deserved it since he'd worked so hard. There we were, broke and deeper and deeper in debt just so the little boy who pretended to be a man Bob could feel good, and there we were driving up for job interviews, and flat broke, in a BMW."

"Typical. Men and cars, you know. At least Monroe doesn't have that flaw. Plenty of others, but not that one."

"I'm still driving the same car I got fifteen years ago when my mother died, and Bob is on his fourth BMW. You know, there's something fatal about the state of mind that tells you to be loyal, to be kind, to be supportive, to be patient and loving, and our patience and love will change the other person. In the end, that state of mind is telling you to be stupid as a post, because now I look back and wonder how and why I ever lived even a day with him."

"It's hard to see things when you're in the middle of them."

"Thank God I've got Earl in my life now, even if there are some things about him that aren't the greatest, like his past, at least he's a good man, and he loves me."

"I hope you're right," Lydia said.

"I am. It's strange though, how this goes all against what we're taught, as women, to believe, because the more I helped Bob and the more patient I was and the more I put up with, and the more strength I provided for both of us, the more he seemed to resent it, and the angrier he got at me. I never understood that."

"Well, you just said it. And you know what it is. They like us weak. I swear they do."

"I despise Bob. And I hate myself for having given so much of myself to someone so utterly unworthy."

"Well, it's over."

"I know, but it haunts me. I don't know when I'll ever get over it. You know when Bob was nicest to me?"

"Of course I do, the same as when any man is nicest to you. When you're weak or feel bad."

"Exactly. I remember when I had my operation for that fibroid thing, and he came to the hospital, and I was just coming out of the anesthesia, and he stood beside my bed, and talked so sweetly to me, and pushed the hair out of my eyes and off my forehead, and within a week, back home, he was screaming and yelling and slamming doors and throwing books again."

"Yep."

"How'd we get into that, anyway?" Martha asked.

"We were talking about states of mind, and like, if there were no men, would you miss them, or, like, do you know what life is supposed to be like, or what you're supposed to be like, if no one tells you, which is what I was thinking about after I saw this movie where there was a girl, and she had this horrible mother, who hated her, and kept her locked away alone. She hated her for her youth or beauty or innocence, or whatever, and the girl, though, who did become sort of strange from being locked up all the time by herself, somehow figured out about life, as if she, or we, are born with this vision of our life already in us, and we try to make it come true from the first day on. Somehow she figured out about life, and, knew in herself what she wanted, what she needed, and, well, to make a long story short, she broke out eventually, and ran away with this older man."

"What movie was that?"

"I can't remember, but the point is, if a person wants to live, she will, and she will do whatever she has to to live, to follow that vision of her life that she has, wherever it came from. She will. She just will."

"How do you explain putting up with the Bobs of the world with that theory?"

"I don't know. Or the Monroes? I don't know. I wish he would come to his senses, though. We are so good, when we're good, I mean, when we're together."

Lydia carefully placed her foot onto her knee, as if she were concentrating on one particular spot.

"My foot's about to go to sleep," she said. "I love the way it feels when your foot falls asleep. It's the kind of nonsense I'm needing about now to take my mind off things. I had this friend in elementary school what used to come over every day in the summer, and we'd play cards and stuff all day long, and make our feet go to sleep. We'd play Ping-Pong for hours, cut out patterns for clothes we'd never make, just anything, always having fun. We used to have contests to see who could make her foot go to sleep first, the only trick was, you couldn't tell if the other person was faking. I never faked it. I don't fake anything."

"I know you don't, Lydia."

"My foot would get so numb it'd scare me. It would feel like it was going to break off. Then I'd try to walk, and it would hurt worse.

"I always wondered if you could damage yourself that way, but I don't think you could. It's probably like holding your breath. Your body wouldn't let you go too far. I wish your mind was like your body. I wish it knew to stop you before you went too far. I wish it could tell you when you were getting ready to make a mistake, or go too far. That'd be nice."

She picked her foot up in the air, and dropped it back onto her knee.

"Let's try to make our feet fall asleep," she said. "Just for the fun of it. Just for the craziness of it. Just so we won't sit here thinking about all the things we might think about, except we don't want to think about, except they keep coming up, except if we were numb then we couldn't think at all. Right? Gosh, I'm talking crazy again, and I'm about to cry and I don't want to cry. I don't. I just want things to be right. I don't want to cry and I don't want to think about anything that I can't do anything about. I just want to sit here until my foot goes so asleep I couldn't move if a crazy person walked through the door."

IT WAS WEDNESDAY EVENING and Mrs. Cutler had invited Monroe for dinner. He had told her Lydia would be visiting her mother, because not only did he not want to get into the fact that he and Lydia were not married, but he didn't want to have to go into why she wasn't really there, because he thought it might interfere with his relationship with Ronnie.

Arkansas was serving, and the good china and sterling were out, and the bell was in front of Mrs. Cutler's plate. The bell made a tiny sound, a refined sound, a delicate sound, and its notice was far different from the ship's bell that brought Ronnie running.

Its ring said, Arkansas, if you please, we are ready, and everything is wonderful, and everything is, and will be, smooth and effortless and proper, and when I ring this bell, you will pause behind the door with the tray in your hands, and then enter.

The door will swing open, and you will enter, carrying the tray, to serve the food. You will remove the previous course as we graciously continue eating. You will then back into the door, gently, on your way to the kitchen, and you will not kick it or slam it against the wall like some people sometimes have, but you will back into it gently, and then disappear.

There will be the silence, and then, the clink, the low steady clink of the fork against the plate, and the knife will glide through the tender meat. The meat will rise into the air, and approach the lips, and conversation will be timed to end before the little section of the dead animal enters the oral cavity.

The lips will close, and there will be the silence as things perfect unfold, and there will be no massive load of food tumbling inside the washing machine-sized mouth.

That is what that tiny, delicate bell was meant to represent.

"Veronica, dear, smile when you talk to the doctor. Don't be so glum."

She was smiling. Oh yes. Inside, she was smiling, and she was thinking, and she was dreaming, and inside she was doing far more smiling than her mother would ever imagine.

"Veronica's manners are sometimes not what we would wish," she said.

Veronica's manners were fine. They were excellent. She knew how to lie still in a tub of hot water. She knew how to allow her legs to fall open, to spread against the sides with her knees up and her thighs red and loose from the heat of the water. She knew how to be still, and how to concentrate, not on the words, but on the feel, on the exquisite feel of a smooth and educated hand as it passed over her.

"Mr. Cutler will have to talk with his daughter later this evening," the enormous woman said, as she and Monroe and the quiet man at the head of the table to Monroe's right, watched Ronnie slide out of her chair and under the table.

"She will listen to her father. At times," the mother said, as Ronnie's hand appeared and found a roll on her plate, and took it under the table with her, where she remained even after the meal was finished, and after everyone else had left the table, and even after her mother kicked through the white linen tablecloth that concealed her, kicked at her, but missed, as if trying to drive a cat from its hiding place. Ronnie stayed there until she heard her father ask Monroe if he'd like to see his rosebushes, and heard her mother trudge upstairs, and then she came out, and ran to the den, where she turned on the TV and paced around in front of it, and tossed a pillow up in the air, again and again, while she tried to live down the embarrassment of the things she'd heard her mother telling Monroe.

"Please excuse my wife," Mr. Cutler said, as he and Monroe walked across the yard. "I'm afraid some of what she said at the table isn't exactly true."

"I understand."

"I don't think you do. You see, Mrs. Cutler has a drinking problem, poor thing, which manifests itself not all of the time, but with regularity, I should say, with enough regularity to cause trouble for everyone involved."

"I wondered about that."

"She's hard on Veronica when she drinks. I'm sorry about that, but there's little I have ever been able to do about it. She had Veronica late in life, you know, too late, some would say, of course we married late, both of us, and we never expected to have children, but it happened, and she never was the same after the birth."

"I see."

"A horrible birthing. It went on for days. The labor, I mean, and I think Mrs. Cutler never recovered from that, at least that's the best I can deduce from it all."

"So Ronnie is your natural child?" Monroe asked.

"Of course she is. Why do you ask?"

"I wasn't sure. I just wondered, that's all."

"I presume you mean because subtracting Veronica's age from what you would guess our ages to be, you saw an unusual configuration, and that's so, but yes, she's our child, even if we've never known quite what to make of her, or what to do with her."

"She's a wonderful girl," Monroe said. "Truly wonderful."

"I know. My heart breaks thinking about what will happen to her as she gets older, leaves home, and so forth. She's been so odd all her life, with few friends, no boyfriends at all that I know of, and always in trouble in whatever school we enrolled her."

"Yes, Ronnie told me she always had trouble in school."

"She's not graduated you know."

"I know that."

"Veronica seems to like you a lot. Quite a lot."

"I like her, too."

"You're not married to Lydia, are you?" the old man asked.

"No, I'm not."

"And has she moved out on you?"

"Yes, actually, she has."

"I thought so."

They walked around the raised beds with the rosebushes neatly arranged in them, six plants, neatly pruned, per neatly mulched and bordered bed.

"And what are your intentions toward Veronica?" Mr. Cutler asked.

"Just friendship," Monroe said. "I enjoy her company."

After they came back inside, Mr. Cutler sent Ronnie upstairs to get her mother so they could all sit together and talk.

"She won't come down. She's got the door locked," Ronnie said.

"Well, leave her be, then," her father said.

"Can we watch a movie on cable?" Ronnie asked.

"Certainly. Go right ahead, but excuse me if I don't join you. I've brought some work home with me to do."

"None of that crap she said about me is true," Ronnie told Monroe when they were alone on the couch in front of the television."

"I know. Your father told me."

"What else did he tell you?"

"Not much. Just casual talk."

"They don't know me, you see."

"I can believe that."

"You know me, though."

"I do," he said, "I think I do."

"The me they talk about is not the me that's really me. Which makes sense because they're not really my parents. Right?"

"If you say so."

An old Roy Rogers film was on television, on cable. Dale Evans was in the film. They could both ride well. Roy's horse, Trigger, and Dale's horse, Buttermilk, were fast. They made clouds of dust as they rode the range. It was obvious how much Roy loved Dale, and she loved him. They did everything together.

In the film, Gabby Hayes owned a cattle ranch.

Dale, an Easterner, had inherited a sheep ranch near-by. Gabby hated sheep. Someone framed Gabby to look like he'd killed the foreman of Dale's ranch. Roy was called in. He worked for the cattlemen's association. He and Dale made a bond. They formed an immediate trust in each other. Gabby was released from jail when Roy discovered the corruption of the bad people. Roy and Dale rode off together. They were going back to Dale's ranch and make love. No one had ever seen them make love before.

In this version of the film, the scene was still there. Ronnie and Monroe watched. First, Dale removed her undergarments. She was wearing a calico skirt, with fringes around the bottom. Below that, she wore calf-height cowgirl boots, and an ornate, fitted cotton shirt.

She removed her undergarments, but put back on the skirt, the blouse, and the boots. Roy liked this. Monroe liked it as well, and thought it would be fun to dress Ronnie like that.

Dale was passionate. This was not something that could have been known for certain before. But she was. The lovemaking went on and on. Roy was in good condition, and was able to do what was required. Then it was over.

Gabby knocked on the door. Roy unlocked the door. Dale was too spent to get out of bed. Once inside, Gabby looked around. He could tell what had occurred. He turned to the camera, and, with a disgusted look on his face and in a grouchy voice, said, "Gall-durned newfangled women."

That was the end of the film.

"Now that's me," Ronnie said.

"I know. I know it is," Monroe told her.

"Don't listen to them. Maybe I didn't graduate, and maybe I did. But who cares?"

"It doesn't matter. In the largest perspective one could take, it matters not at all. And anyway," he told her, and pulled her close, "what matters to me is Lydia's gone. Gone, you see. Finally gone."

"Can I move in with you yet?"

"No. But soon."

"All right," she said.

"I feel so good. I feel better than I have in years. In a long time, at least. Certainly, in a very, long time."

"So do I."

They talked quietly. Mr. Cutler had retired to his wing, and Mrs. Cutler was upstairs. They thought Monroe was counseling Ronnie.

"Can I come over tonight?" she asked.

"No. I have to get up early."

"Darnit."

It was raining outside. It rained hard, and steadily. It rained with great force, and had been like this ever since Monroe followed the dark-skinned woman into the parking lot. The sound of the rain was comforting. Monroe and Ronnie huddled together, as if they were braving a storm, or making a crossing, or stranded in a car in such a fierce storm they could not see to drive, but had to stop, and hold each other.

"I could come over for a little while," she said. "But not stay all night."

"No. Do as I say, Ronnie. Wait until I tell you."

"All right."

The wind blew. The trees bent. Dead branches fell, and green leaves littered the street. A porch swing swung, no one in it. Rocking chairs rocked, and a plaster figurine, with pastel colored clothes, and a hat, and a parasol, blew off the window above the kitchen sink in Monroe's house.

It hit the ledge of the cast iron, enameled sink,

broke, and fell in pieces into the skillet below. The skillet was full of water. In the water, flakes of scrambled eggs from breakfast floated. The pieces of the figurine floated, and the head bobbed like a cork, and then sank. The water filled the cavity of the plaster skull through a hole poked into the female figurine's lips.

The hole had been opened through the lips to allow the heat to escape when the figurine was fired, but it also gave the shy, Victorian female a startled look. She looked as if she'd seen something that surprised her, something naughty. Her mouth was open, as if she were saying, Oh, after having been asked to do something she'd never considered before, and she was about to lose her innocence.

The long, pastel skirt, the buttoned-up ankle boots, the bodice fastened all the way to her neck, the hat primly in place, and the parasol to protect her, would no longer help. The expression on her face, the startled look, the parted lips, clearly indicated she was interested, and would say, yes.

LYDIA'S FOOT WAS TOO numb to move when Earl came home drunk, and Martha herself had to hobble along beside him, helping him into bed.

"I'm going somewhere, anyway," Lydia said.

"You don't have to. He's going to sleep the rest of the night."

"He didn't the last time."

"He was upset about something. That's what you heard. We weren't, I mean, it wasn't a fight."

"I'm going out, though, because I've got an idea, and I want to act on it."

It continued raining. Lydia's wipers did not work well. The blades, the rubber component of the wipers, were brittle and smeared the windshield. The springs of the wiper arms were weak, and the arms lifted up, and hydroplaned on the film of water.

Deep puddles formed. Narrow torrents rushed against the curb and gutters. The water was too much for the storm drains. It overflowed.

Lydia's car, but not only hers, going too fast for

conditions, splashed through these puddles. Her car, and others with old wires, or weak spark, or cracks in the cap or coil, drowned from the volume of water splashed into the engine.

Cars stopped. Police with flashing lights pulled behind one or the other to warn away traffic. Lydia coasted into a parking lot. She waited for the rain to abate, and for the heat of the engine to dry the wires. She locked the doors. There were crazy people everywhere. Angry people. A woman, alone, really did have to be careful.

IN MONROE AND Lydia's rented house were two permanently locked rooms, and Lydia had always wanted to get in these rooms, and Monroe had never allowed it.

The doors opened out. Most closet doors, and some doors to other rooms, opened out, but mostly, doors opened inward. When doors opened out, the molding stop that shielded the latch and prevented the door from swinging past center was on the inside, and the latch was exposed. That meant that though the knob was locked and would not turn, the latch itself could be forced back by a screwdriver or other thin device.

One of these doors was to a closet. The other to a bedroom. It was unusual for a bedroom to open out, and for the locking part of the knob to be on the outside.

There could be reasons for this. One reason was that an amateur hung the door improperly. Another was to facilitate locking someone in the room, if necessary. A man on the coast once locked his wife in their bathroom this way, and left her for dead. It happened.

Suppose, given the nature of people, once they were alone with each other, inside their homes, out of sight, suppose this were the case.

A husband might have a wife who was disobedient. Maybe she talked back. Maybe she failed to clean the house. Maybe she burned the dinner, or would not have sex on demand, or demanded it herself one too many times. Naturally, these things would have occurred in the past, before modern times, when people began to understand one another better, so possibly the door was hung with the lock to the outside, because of that.

It was possible, then, when Monroe entered this bedroom, with its double bed still made, and the furniture still in place, and the mirror over the dresser but nothing on the dresser, it was possible, then, that in this house, which had the same furniture and the same decor and the same feel of all the houses he had grown up in after the end of the war, after the men came home and the women were taught what to do, and what not to do, it was possible that this mother, this wife, had not been a good mother and a good wife, and that, on occasion, she had been required to go to her room, and had been locked in until she could decide to behave.

There was a window. Because there was a window, it would be unlikely that anyone could have actually been locked in here. A person could crawl out the window.

Well, it was a second-floor window. Desperate enough, she might have jumped. She might have been injured. The neighbors might have seen her. Then it would be known. It would be known she was crazy, and trying to kill herself, or she would have to tell them about her life.

She would have to tell them that sometimes she was locked in the room because she would not cooperate, or because she had lacked patience, and had asked for something women didn't ask for, but merely waited for, being good, being quiet, being still, waiting, like they were supposed to. Back then.

She would either tell them about that, or hang her head and admit she had tried to kill herself. So, the window did not matter. It did not matter at all. It could have been on the first floor and been the same.

"Hi," Lydia said.

Monroe had not heard her enter the house, nor heard her on the stairs.

"You scared me," he said. "How long have you been there?"

"Not long. I phoned earlier. I let it ring and ring."

"I was out."

"I thought you might be, but then again, with the rain like it is, I wondered if you were at home, and maybe feeling blue, and not answering the phone."

"It only began raining a while ago."

"It's been raining for days, Monroe."

"No, it hasn't."

"Where were you, anyway?"

"I went out. To eat."

"I wish you'd called. We could have had supper together."

"I'm sorry. I didn't think of it."

"Gosh, I've missed you," she said.

"You have?"

That was the wrong response. Even if he did not mean it, when she said, gosh, I've missed you, or said, as she might, I love you, he should have said, I've been missing you, too, or, I love you, too. It was supposed to be automatic. In some people, who've been trained right, it was. One did not say, in a flat voice, with one's eyes looking at anything but her, you have?

"Why are you in this room?" she asked.

"I do not know."

"Did the people come by, and open it?"

"No."

"Then how did you get in?"

"With a screwdriver."

"But why?"

"I do not know. It's a strange room. It's like my parents' room was. Same kind of furniture."

"Mine, too."

"Sit down," he said, and patted beside him.

"I looked all around for you, downstairs," she said. "I had no idea you had went in here."

"Bored, I guess."

"What about that other room?"

"It's a closet. I already opened it."

"Let's go see," she said.

There were old clothes. There were boxes. In the boxes were letters, photographs, old hats, shoes, and souvenirs from travels and from the war.

Most of the letters were from the war. The man missed his wife, terribly. He wrote in a formal style, and never said anything crude, but it was obvious he longed for her, and hated his life overseas, and wanted to return. It was evident from these letters that the lock on the bedroom door could not have been put there by this husband in order to contain this wife. The best reason the lock was backwards was so the heirs could lock the tenants out of these two rooms.

"I wonder what life was like in this house, as the man and woman grew older, and the family left."

"It could be anything," he said.

"I bet it was nice. The way they've saved everything and not sold the house, it's as if they want to remember the way it was."

"Possibly."

"I like the way they looked," she said, holding up a photograph.

"They do look nice."

"There must have been something good here, the way they stayed together, and raised their family."

"Yes."

"Look at these shoes," she said. "I would loved to have lived back then, to wear clothes like these."

"Put them on," he said.

"A dead person's shoes?"

"Are you afraid to?" he asked.

"Of course not. How do I look?"

"Very nice."

"They'd look better if I wore a dress, than with these pants."

"Find one," he said. "Wear one of these."

"You go out for a minute. Go in the other room."

She dressed up, and then walked in, slowly, as if on stage.

"It's amazing," he said. "I always like that thirties, forties, whatever it was, look myself."

"Why don't you find something of his, and put it on."

"No, thanks."

"Oh, go ahead. It'd be fun. Do it. Please."

"Why should I?"

"Because you owe it to me."

"How's that?"

"I mean, you owe it to me, and to yourself, and to us. You owe it to yourself, really, most of all, to be as much fun as you used to be. I'm sorry," she said. "I had no right to say that."

"It's interesting you did, though."

"Forget it. You don't owe me a thing. You only owe yourself whatever it is that you want. I guess that's the only truth about it."

"You want to play, though. Right? Is that what it is? You want to play, like we used to, and see if it's still there."

"Oh, Lord," she said. "Now I do wish I hadn't said it."

"I think you're on to something."

"Just forget it. Putting it into words makes it sound awful."

23

IN MARTHA'S APARTMENT, EARL sat on the edge of the bed, the same as Monroe had when Lydia found him upstairs. Earl stared out the window at the rain. Martha was face down in a tangle of sheets.

He went into the kitchen. On the way he passed Selby, who was visiting for a few days, asleep on the couch. He removed a pan, filled it with water, and put it on the stove. Only one burner worked. He tried one after the other, feeling the circular elements, until he found the one that worked.

The door to the oven was partly open. The two springs attached to its hinges were broken. Because of this, the door would not stay closed. When they baked, they had to prop the door shut, with a chair.

There was a puddle of water seeping out from under the refrigerator. The refrigerator was modern, and came with the apartment. It was self-defrosting. In most of these models, a pan sits under a drip tube, and when the defrosting surge cycles on, the water collects in this pan, and then evaporates from the force of the fan blowing hot air across it.

The pan was missing from this refrigerator. Because it was missing, the water dripped from the tube onto the floor. It was not much water. It was about the amount there would be if one spilled a coffee cup. It felt awful to forget the water was there and step barefoot into it.

The water on the stove boiled. Earl couldn't find the instant coffee. The only coffee he could find was sweet, blended coffee with a European name. He fixed it, and tasted it. He spit it on the floor, poured it out, and threw the can across the room.

He roused his friend. Selby stretched, and rubbed his eyes, and followed him.

Martha was glad Lydia was out for the evening, because now that Earl had finished with her, he was getting ready to turn her over to his friend. That is, literally speaking, he turned her over, and left the room, and now Selby was about to use her, that way.

Selby had been waiting in the other room. That was nice of him, and showed politeness and courtesy. An unpleasant man might have actually been waiting in the same room. But Selby showed he knew how to be decent, and appreciative, and only entered the room after Earl told him he could.

The man showed even further how well he understood women, and that he cared for their feelings, because, before he began, he spoke to her.

"You ready?" he asked.

Other men, in that same situation, with a woman waiting in that position, and having been given permission by the man in charge of her, might have gone right to it. This fellow knew enough about women to realize that the kind words and the tender moments before the actual event were important, and because of this, upon arriving in the room, he spoke to her, and pushed her on the shoulder, as if trying to wake her.

"You ready?"

No one could accuse men of not having learned that it was more than sex itself that women wanted, and even rougher, less educated types such as Selby now knew about it, and so, he spoke to her.

"You ready?"

"WELL, THAT WAS FUN, after all," Lydia said.

"I enjoyed it myself," Monroe said.

They had returned from a late-night dessert at a fancy restaurant. They had both dressed in the old clothes. Monroe treated her in a courtly manner, and she got into acting as if she were a shy, new bride.

"I dare say we made quite a show," she said.

"I dare say, my dear, you are correct."

"Some of the people, though, what saw us, didn't hardly know what to make of it."

"True. They didn't hardly know what. That's probably true."

"But you know, my good man," she said. "I certainly did. It felt so good, being loose again, and acting foolish, and all like that."

"You had fun, then?"

"I did. Truly, I did," she said, and kissed him on the cheek.

"It does not seem to take much," he said.

"Take much for what?"

"It seems to be easy to make you happy."

"Oh, it is. It-is-it-is-it-is," she said, as rapidly as she could run the words together. "That's so true. Simple things make me happy, and real things, and fun. Anything fun. You know that."

"I do know that. Yes. I do."

"And kissing, too," she said, and kissed him on the lips this time. "That always makes me happy. Maybe the happiest, because, you know, it's kind of the dessert to the day, or the icing, or whatever you could call it. It's the wrap-up, or something."

"The wrap-up," he said.

"Oh, whatever. You know I'm not good with words. But I know what I like."

Monroe went upstairs to remove the old man's clothes, and return them to the closet, while Lydia showered. Then he came back down dressed in what he'd been wearing during the day.

He turned on the television. A radio was on in another room. Lydia was singing. The phone rang.

"You're on the air, live, with Gee-One-Oh-Nine," someone said.

Monroe hung up. He flipped across the channels. The phone rang again.

"We were disconnected. You are on the air, live, with Gee-One-Oh-Nine," the voice said, "and if you correctly identify the artist for our next song, we'll send you one hundred and nine dollars, good American cash."

"Go suck yourself," Monroe told him, and hung up.

"Who was that? Didn't we just get two calls?" Lydia asked.

"A radio station."

"Well, gosh," she said, "was it the one I was listening to? They have contests all the time."

"I don't know."

"Who was it? Was it the Night Caller, that guy who calls himself that?"

"I don't know."

"Was it Bobby Rex?"

"I don't know."

"Well, we don't need to be bothered. You're right. Not tonight. I was thinking how we should have stayed dressed up longer, and figured out, like, what they would have been doing this time of night, say, on this date, about forty years ago."

"One does, right away, think there'd be no television," he said.

"Oh, right. Would they have listened to the radio?"

"They might."

"Or just talk. Just talk to each other?"

"Possibly."

"What would people have talked about back then?"

"Who knows. The war. Probably the war. It would have been over four years earlier. Everyone would have come home, and started to live the way they were supposed to live."

"Yes, they'd be talking about that, I guess. And what else? Like whether they'd have children, or not?"

"Everyone wanted children back then," he said.

"Oh, yes. Maybe they'd talk about how many they'd have."

"Maybe."

"And then, ummmmm, what else?"

"I don't know."

"There must have been something."

"Probably the men did the talking, and the women listened."

"I don't think that's right."

"You said your father came home and told you stories about his life and the things he'd done during the day."

"Yes."

"Did your mother talk?"

"Well, she did. I think she did. To us, but maybe not so much to him. I guess she didn't. Or, maybe she did, but not around us."

"I see."

"Something's wrong, isn't it?" she asked.

"Not really."

"But ever since I came back in, after my shower, you've been acting different. I mean, we've been talking, but you haven't looked at me. Why won't you look at me?"

"Here we go again," he said.

"But it's such a clear night-and-day thing. I mean, I go out of the room, and come back, and it's like I'm a stranger, that fast."

"I wondered how long it'd be, before it slipped back, all the way, no less."

"Well, I have a right to know."

"You want to know? You really want to know?"

"Yes."

"Even though you won't like it, you want to know?"

"I do, because I have to know."

"Well, Lydia, it's very simple. You see what I'm wearing?"

"Yes."

"These are clothes. These are what's called street clothes."

"So?"

"And what are you wearing?"

"This?"

"Yes, that."

"My nightgown."

"Right. And who, pray tell, said anything about your spending the night here? Who?"

"But, I thought . . ."

"I know you did. You have a one-track mind, poor thing. It's amazing how I feel sorry for you, and despise you at the same time."

"But, I thought, after all the fun we'd had."

"I know that's what you thought, because it's what you *would* think. You see. It's what you would think, and who, I ask you, who said anything, one word, even, about you and me sleeping together."

"Oh, gosh, oh, Lord," she sighed, "this can't be happening."

"It is, though. You're like a one-trick pony, you know. That's essentially what you are. A one-trick pony."

"And what do you mean by that? Tell me what you mean by that, if you have the nerve."

"It means you only have one trick, Lydia, and that's getting a man in bed with you, and that's about it."

She got out of the chair, and walked around the room in a circle, shaking her head, pulling her hair over her eyes, going blind, going mad.

"I might as well be dead," she said.

"That's not necessary."

"Look, Monroe, I'm trying to stay calm. I'd like to explain something to you, and then I'll leave. You see, I'm just a person. Just a human being. A normal, regular person, with normal thoughts and normal needs, and just the run-of-the-mill, good old-fashioned, normal feelings one person might have for another.

Can you understand that? And sometimes, being a normal, everyday person, I get to thinking that someone else might feel the same way I feel, and then I guess that's where I make my mistake, because then it turns out they don't, and look where I'm left. Out here, alone, like a damn fool."

"Not a fool, Lydia, just a person who goes too far. That's all."

"I guess, I see now, that I was wrong. I guess I was. It's hard to admit it, but I thought, for instance, that you might be lonely. I was lonely. I was lonely for you. I thought you might be feeling the same way."

"Well," he said, "the point of that is, that for you, lonely doesn't mean what it might for someone else. For you, it's different. For you, lonely is a synonym for needing sex."

IT HAD BEEN A busy month in the emergency room. The amount of injury, trouble, and self-induced terror that they were seeing would either prove to be a blip on a chart or the beginning of a new era. Monroe worked extra days each week. He signed on for this extra duty to make as much money as possible in as short a time as possible, because he was contemplating resigning his position at the hospital. At his rate of pay, he was able to earn enough in a few extra days each week to last a long time, should he actually resign.

One afternoon, resting in the room reserved for the doctors to relax and nap in, Monroe and his colleague talked about their lives, and the women in their lives, and Monroe remembered an incident he hadn't thought of in a long time.

"I was with this woman," he began, but the other doctor interrupted him.

"Was this before or after Lydia?"

"Before Lydia, after Katy."

"Okay."

"And we went back to her apartment, and she

was a bit tense, and I liked her, all right, and felt like it would be nice to be with her that night, to be close, as they call it, you know, let's be close, they say, and you know what they mean when they say that, and so I sat beside her on the couch and put my arm around her, and kissed her on her cheek, and on her neck, and then I put my hand across her belly, not on her breasts, or between her legs, but across her belly, and she said, no. No, she said, don't do that, because I have to know a man better, and have to trust him, before I can do what you're probably thinking.

"So I said, then, can we just kiss? Can we just kiss a little? Would that be all right? And she said, sure, I would like that. So we began to kiss, and after a few minutes, she arched up in the air, and turned toward me, and started kissing *me*, and then a few minutes later, no more than ten minutes after it all started, she started gasping, and saying, over and over, Oh god, I trust you, I trust you, which she then repeated, gaspingly, into my ear, over and over, all the while grabbing all over me, and then she pulled me off the couch, and onto the floor, I trust you, she kept saying, I trust you, I do, I do, I do, she said, and I was trying to get my bearings, and she rolled us onto the floor, and got herself under me, and was trying to get into whatever position she needed to be in, to get her pelvic region aligned the way she wanted it with mine, I suppose, and she started pulling me around, and moving me around on her, and we started across the floor, and were bunching up this rug she had on the wood floor, a throw rug, and we bunched that up awhile," he said, and paused, as the other doctor wiped the tears from his eyes from laughing so much, "and then she had us moving toward this coffee table, and I grabbed hold of the leg of the couch, and she was digging her heels into the floor and throwing me up and down, I trust you, I trust you, she said, rocking her head back and forth, out of her mind, and she was pushing so hard, trying to get the way she wanted, pretty soon she was pulling the couch, and me, and the bunched-up rug, all the way across the floor, and we rolled, or undulated, you might say, into the coffee table, and knocked it over, and then she started back the other way, and by the time it was all over, we were under, mind you, under the couch, which somehow she'd tipped up onto its back legs, and got me under it, on top of her, at which point, I suppose, the weight of the couch and the enforced position of us against it, brought her off, thank god, and she finally relaxed and let go of me, and I lay there awhile, mentally examining myself for injury, and finally we crawled out, and had some coffee, and I went home."

26

MARTHA AND EARL OPENED a bar. Martha cooked, and Earl ran the bar and acted as bouncer, and Selby hung around, doing whatever was necessary.

Lydia attended the grand opening, but did not return until Martha asked her to take her home early one evening. On that evening, Earl had booked a group of lady mud wrestlers, but the main event for the night, which Lydia hoped she would see, just out of curiosity, was an old-fashioned knife-throwing act.

In the act, the woman was strapped to a circular board. The board then went around and around, like a wheel, and the man threw the knives at the woman strapped in place.

It was a huge success, and the couple, the man and woman in the act, who were actually married, were asked to perform again the next night.

The audience, which was raucous and obscene during the mud wrestling, was quiet and reflective for the knife act. There was a deep shared reverence for the woman's willingness to be strapped down, and for her courage, and for the skill of the man to throw the knives, and nearly kill her, so that, by the end of the act, the woman would have offered herself, given herself to the man, and said, in essence, I am yours, kill me if that's what you want, but then, like all good endings, she survived, if only to do it again the next night.

It was eerie to be a part of the silent men, watching the ritualization of control, and of punishment, of sacrifice and offering, and it gave Lydia the worst feeling of her life.

"I am never going in there again," she told Martha. "I don't mean it in a bad way for you, but listen, girl, that place is just creepy. Really creepy."

"It brings in the money. A lot of it."

"But those acts. The mud wrestling. The knife act."

"But you see, they're just acts. That's all. The guys sit there, like they do when we have topless night, and they dream about god only knows what, and sometimes they yell and scream and whoop and holler, but nothing really bad ever happens."

"Did you see the woman's face? On the board? Just before he strapped her down."

"You don't want to look at their faces. I mean, honestly, you never want to look in their eyes. Half of them are totally strung out on drugs, which is how they got the jobs in the first place. Especially the topless dancers. When they arrive, it's like a drugstore back there."

"It's awful."

"Even the mud wrestlers, they're usually dykes, but some of them are on something, I think. I don't know what."

"The woman tonight, though," Lydia said, "really

got to me. She looked sad. She just looked sad, all the way, through and through."

"We're paying them two hundred dollars for about an hour's worth of work. Two shows per night, two hundred dollars per night. That's not bad."

"It's still bizarre."

"Lydia, it's just an act. That's your trouble. You get reality confused with acts. You do it all the time."

APARTMENTS ARE CONSTRUCTED BETTER than they used to be. The walls between the units must be thick. These walls are called firebreaks, and often employ the use of twelve-inch masonry blocks. Sometimes, it is easier, faster, and cheaper to use a standard framed wall, and layer the supports with multiple pieces of five-eighths of an inch fire-resistant drywall. This achieves the same purpose, and either method meets the building code, and is relatively soundproof.

It is difficult, if not impossible, for a normal man, or woman, to punch a fist through multiple layers of five-eighths of an inch fire-code drywall. Therefore, even the apartments where the drunks and violent people lived usually had intact the walls that separated them from the other units.

It's easy, though, to punch one's fist through the single layer of half-inch drywall that covered the partitions within the apartments, such as the walls between the bathroom and the bedroom, or between one bedroom and another.

Even with holes in these partition walls, because of the newer construction methods of the frame or concrete forms and the firebreaks themselvés, these units were substantial, compared to what might have been. Had there been no fire codes, however, the walls between the units might, too, be full of holes, and then, anyone next door could know what life was really like for their neighbors.

Because certain things cost money in construction, and because land was expensive, and because most multi-family projects were set up on a seven-year payback for the investors, there had to be some place to save money, and that place was in the fixtures, and the appliances, and the hardware, and the lighting, and the carpeting and the vinyl, and the use of hollow-core doors, aluminum windows, and prefabricated countertops and cabinets.

The countertop, where Martha warmed a late supper for herself and Lydia, had peeled. This was the same counter that contacted the oven, which only had one working burner, and whose door would not close by itself, and which, on the other end, nudged the refrigerator that dripped onto the floor.

Where the countertop had peeled was a strange-looking, compressed mass of sawdust and glue, known as particle board. Martha set the hot container onto this, and it burned it. The smell of the burning formaldehyde, which was in the glue, and the sawdust itself, was horrible, and they decided to go out to dinner.

Martha went to the bathroom to wash up before they left. The toilet rocked back and forth on the loose tile floor. When it did, it squished, like the sound of a damp sponge, squeezed and released, squeezed and released. The roll of paper was on the floor. Imprinted on the first few layers, was a sampling of everyone's hair who had recently used the bathroom. She peeled away the layers until she found a clean part of the roll. She put the roll on the wooden coaster on the tank.

Behind the curtain, in the shower, a roach slid down the wall. It was moving fast, like a child zipping down a sliding board, and it was on its way to get a drink of water from the puddle in the bottom of the tub, which collected from the drip of the faucets, and which never completely drained, because of the slant of the tub, which was to the rear, instead of toward the drain, due to the settling of the floor.

Martha changed clothes. Lydia heard her slamming the closet door. The doors, bypass or track doors, had been one of the last items negotiated in the price of the units by the builders. They had located, after many phone calls, a reasonably priced set. These doors, which would only slide to one side if you wrapped your arms around them and carried them there, also fell off the track if you released them too quickly, so that, essentially, each time you used them you had to rehang them, and you could not merely leave them open, because one or the other was always blocking one or the other side of the closet.

Martha returned to the bathroom, and flushed the toilet once more. As the water evacuated the bowl, a film of what was on its way down seeped onto the floor. She did not look. She knew it happened. She did not look. She did not even look in the mirror on the way out, because she did not want to see her hair, which she had cheaply dyed glossy, shoe polish black.

ON A RARE DAY off from work, Monroe read through a stack of newspapers he had missed when they were current. From among the papers, there were four unusually interesting articles.

In one, an educated man, a lawyer, had beaten his daughter to death. His wife, an editor for a company that published children's books, had known about her daughter's beatings, and had allowed them to continue. The article said the husband had beaten his wife over the years, and the beatings, many of them sexually inspired, were never reported by the woman. The daughter had finally died, and therefore, ended it all. Her death exposed the man, the woman, and the entire situation.

Tenants of the building where this family lived expressed the outrage any sane person would feel. One man said he hoped the lawyer would end up in prison for the rest of his life, where, he said, he would find out what rough sex was all about, and would find out what beatings were all about, and would discover what real rage was all about.

In another article, an extremist group in a large, northern city was advocating that all men, after a certain age, such as eighteen or twenty-one, the actual plateau had not been determined, would be required to have their sexual organ measured, and that these measurements would become a matter of public record. The article went on to say there was consensus among experts that the idea would never be made into law, but the group was adamant about the effectiveness of such information becoming a matter of public record.

In the next article, a woman had been jogging in a park. She had been attacked by a group of little boys. These boys, some of them ten years old, a few of them twelve, thirteen, one of them fourteen, had beaten this woman badly, and all of them had sex with her while she lay bleeding.

In the last article Monroe read that day, a well-bred young man had been making love with a girl from similarly privileged circumstances. They had been in a park, after partying at a nightclub. The woman had been found the next morning, according to police reports, strangled to death, with her neck broken.

The young man, who was arrested, made a statement about the accidental nature of the event, and said that he had not even been interested in having sex with her, but that she insisted, and became violent in her insistence, and he had merely done it to please her, and calm her down.

The next day, his lawyer commented that it was entirely and appropriately believable, given the bizarre passion of women nowadays, that she might have broken her own neck, and strangled her own self, while in the act of making love.

The lawyer also said his client had merely been

trying, much like many other men this day and time, to satisfy the extreme, and often brutal needs of these women, and that, far from being the murderer in this episode, the young man had actually been the victim, much as other men, the lawyer said, found themselves to be victimized by the sexual behavior of certain women.

Monroe finished the articles, and then fell asleep. When he awoke, he took them outside to the trash cans. He looked back toward the house. The old place was beautifully landscaped, but not since he moved in had anything been done except mowing the lawn. They had neglected the shrubs and flower beds and ornamentals.

In the front of the house, and along the sides, were holly bushes, which remained green the year round. The leaves were prickly, and they produced abundant red berries each year, and grew rapidly. From each bush now sprouted long, runaway stems. The stems grew straight up, and some of them were three feet above the rounded crown of the bush. Monroe found the clippers in the shed, and snipped them off level with the rest of the bush, and then gathered the prunings, and laid them in a pile in the far corner of the yard.

Next door, Ernest watched Monroe work. Ernest was on his knees, tending to the raised, bordered flower beds, and he could see Monroe through the thin places in the hedge. He watched him wander back and forth among the bushes, snipping a bit here, a bit there, carrying two or three sprigs at a time to the pile in the back, and he did not understand the randomness of Monroe's method.

Ernest watched him the whole time he worked. He was in the shade, in the shadows, and he did not want to rush this job because he could rest his old legs and stay out of the sun, and so he was still there when he saw Ronnie run through the hedge and right into Monroe's arms.

That night, in their yard, before sunset, sitting under the tree beside the house, Ernest and Arkansas sipped iced tea, watched the traffic, listened to the tree frogs and crickets winding up, and enjoyed the peacefulness of the end of the day and the mellow feeling they always had knowing they would be in church the next day, among friends, giving thanks, better understanding the troubles of this world, and praying for those who needed it.

"She jumped up on him," Ernest said.

"I've seen her do that before."

"She run like a little rabbit, a hippity-hoppity, just a-tearing along, and she jumped into his arms and wrapped herself around him so hard he fell over backward."

"And him old enough to be her father," Arkansas said.

"It ain't especially the age what bothers me, to tell you the truth. It's more the kind of man he seem to be. He don't look right. You think he's cross-eyed?"

"No. Not, cross-eyed, but I know what you mean. There is something with his eyes, something not right."

"There sure is."

"And that little Ronnie, she's such a child, such a wild thing, there's no predicting what will come of her."

"It is the Lord's way, sometime, to have you learn it for yourself."

"Amen," she said.

"I feel like a-talking to her sometime. But I don't know what to say."

"It isn't our place to tell white folks how to live. All the changes there are in the world, it still isn't."

"I love that little gal," he said. "I do hate to see her take the wrong path."

"She'll be fine. I do believe she'll be fine, come what may."

Behind them was a line of mimosa trees, exotic and mysterious, that they had planted when they bought the house. In the front corner were two magnolias, side by side, and the tree under which they sat was a weeping willow, in which they had cut out a spot for the chairs and the table. Throughout the yard were trees and plants of every variety, and they all thrived.

Behind the house, behind the shed, where the lawn mower and tools were kept, and the old canning jars were stored when empty, and the trace and harness from the old mule hung on nails in the back wall, behind that wall was an old car. It was hard to see this car from the road, but it was there, and had been there for many years.

From where they sat, under the tree, they could see a little girl approaching this car. She approached it cautiously, stepping through the weeds and poking in front of her with a stick. She was talking to someone, or something, to the car maybe, or to the unknown creatures hiding in the weeds, and she craned her neck this way and that, trying to discern what lay ahead, and what might, or might not, be in the car.

"Go tell that child to stay away from that car," Arkansas said. "You know it's full of snakes."

Ernest got up and walked across the yard to warn

the little girl. He didn't want to yell at her because it would frighten her, and he didn't want to run her off, but just warn her about the snakes. She was a sweet little girl, and it would have broken his heart if she'd been hurt.

IT WAS DIFFICULT TO decide what to do with people you disliked. If you hated certain people, that meant they were important to you, and that probably meant you would rather love them.

If you disliked your mother, or your father, you likely had good reason, because children will forgive anything, again and again, hoping they'd misunderstood, or that what happened was a mistake.

No one who loved you treated you badly. Being treated badly by people was reason enough to hate them, although recently it had been discovered hating people gave you cancer, and so hating someone who hated you and made your life hell, played into their hands.

It was complicated. Lydia hated Monroe, but she hated him only because she could no longer love him, and she could no longer love him because of how badly he'd treated her when she'd been fool enough to think he loved her back.

Ronnie hated her mother, but wished she did not, and even when she had thoughts of violent death and punishment toward the woman, she later felt bad about it, and knew it was wrong. Why people treated each other badly was still a mystery, and the mystery continued on past the point of science and technology and learned minds.

Often one found oneself in situations that brought back the feelings of love, of childhood, of being cared for, of being protected, and nothing felt any better. Years ago, Ronnie was running through the yard, carrying a stick, playing Indian. She fell. The stick went into her throat, just below her chin. It stuck into her so deeply that when she ran toward her house, the stick hung from her, buried like an arrow.

Her mother and her father rushed toward her. They ran toward each other, and their hearts were all the same. Her father carried her to the car, and put her in the back seat, in her mother's arms. Her mother held her, and rocked her, and covered Ronnie's eyes with her comforting hand, and her mother cried with the pain of the arrow, deep in her, as surely as it was in her daughter.

On the way home from the hospital, Ronnie slept, alone, in the back seat, while her mother rode quietly, praying and giving thanks, in the front, reaching back and patting her as they drove slowly, braking with such care, with a precious, live child in the back seat.

The feeling of being cared for, of being protected, returned to Ronnie this day, as she rode in the back seat with her father driving and her mother quietly beside him. She felt safe, as they drove from town into the country to buy fresh peaches from an orchard they visited each and every year.

Ronnie leaned against the window on the passenger side behind her mother, and she looked, for all who might have noticed, like a young child, slumped down, and wide-eyed, and dreamy.

Ahead, around a curve, and half a mile down a straightaway, she saw a pickup truck pull from a county-operated trash site that had three green, open-topped dumpsters side by side. As the pickup passed, Ronnie saw two tough-looking women staring straight ahead, and in the back of the truck, half a dozen empty garbage cans clanged and rolled and bounced off the sides.

Then, as she neared the dumpster site, Ronnie saw a man in one. He was deep in the trash. Only his head and shoulders remained above the top of the dumpster. His face was filthy, and he looked forlorn, tired and confused. There was no car there for him to leave the site, and it appeared that he had been thrown away by the two women in the truck.

Maybe they'd gotten tired of him. Maybe he couldn't do for them what he'd promised, whatever it had been. Maybe they'd felt mean, and took him for a ride, and threw him out, along with everything else they'd finished with.

In one hand, he held a pole. It looked like a broom handle. Ronnie could see the top of the pole where he grasped it. He peered out at them with the saddest expression, as if he was not certain he could actually get out, or as if he had come to believe he must remain there until the lift truck dumped him in, and hauled him away.

"Why is that man in there?" Ronnie asked.

"He's looking for things," her father said. "He's looking for aluminum cans and other objects he might sell."

"I think the people in that truck threw him away."

"No, Veronica. They did not do that. He's merely looking for cans."

Ronnie turned around in the seat, and watched him as long as she could see him. He was in the same spot, and was not looking for cans as far as she could tell, so it truly did appear that he'd been thrown away or abandoned. He turned his head as the car passed, and watched them leave.

She waved to him through the back window. She waved at him as long as she could see him, and then some more.

"We must stop, on the way back," she said. "I want to talk to that man."

LYDIA AND MARTHA FOUND a restaurant in which they were certain they would not accidentally see Monroe. It was small. It had five tables down the middle. Along the walls, on either side of the tables, were booths. The booths were full, and only the tables were vacant.

"I don't mind," Lydia said. "Let's sit anywhere and order. I'm actually hungry."

The food came quickly. It was dark in the room. Each table had a lamp above it. On the table were candles. The candles swam in a pool of oil, or melted wax, and a small flame burned in the middle of the pool. They gave off a smell, like incense.

In a corner booth, in front of Lydia, a man and a woman occupied the same side of the booth. No one sat on the bench across from them. The man had his arm around the woman. She seemed rigid, as if she had not wanted to come along, or wished she were elsewhere, or was upset about something, and had determined she would get through the evening by being still and quiet. The man with his arm around her was eating, and talking to her, and eating some more, and motioning for her to eat, but she remained still.

"That woman's not eating a thing," she said.

"Who?"

"Behind you. Don't look. I can barely see her, but she's sitting with this guy, and she won't even look at him."

"They must be having an argument."

"She is the strangest-looking creature I have seen. She looks like one of those women in your bar. I don't know what she's done to herself, but something's wrong."

While Lydia watched, the man undid the top three buttons of the woman's blouse, and reached his hand inside.

"Uh oh," Lydia said.

"What now?"

"He's got his hand in her blouse."

"What do you mean, in her blouse?"

"I mean, he's rubbing her with his hand."

"What's she doing about it?"

"Sitting there with the same expression on her face, as if it weren't happening."

"I have to see this."

"Don't turn around. He just looked up, and almost saw me watching."

"What's she doing?"

"Nothing."

"Eating?"

"Nothing. She has not moved."

"Some fun."

They ordered dessert. Both had coffee. Lydia watched the man and the woman, but she did it from behind her coffee cup as she drank.

"Oh, gosh," she said. "He just pulled her back and stuck his tongue in her ear."

"I've got to see. I'm moving to your side."

"No. Don't. The guy's getting a crazy look on his face. He might come over here."

Suddenly, the man slapped the woman in the face. Just before he slapped her, he gripped her chin, and squeezed it hard, and tried to bend her head so she would look at him, and when he could not make her turn his way, he slapped her in such a way that if she wanted to avoid the blow, she would have to turn his way.

"He just hit her."

"Hard?"

"Hard enough."

"Let's leave."

"We can't leave. We have to do something."

No one else paid any attention to the man and the woman, and Lydia could not gain support from anyone, by eye contact, for any kind of action.

Soon after the slap, the man took the woman's fork, speared a piece of meat and a vegetable off her plate, and began to force it into her mouth. He first worked his thumb and forefinger on each side of her jaw, and attempted to pry open her mouth, and, at the same time, pushed the fork against her lips and teeth. The woman remained exactly as she was, never moved, never made a sound, but did manage to keep her jaw clenched and her lips together.

Then the man slung the fork into the wall, beside the booth, and took out his wallet, set some money on the table, and walked out the door.

The woman remained still. The only movement Lydia saw was her bottom lip. It shook a little, and, as she watched it shake, a drop of blood fell, like a tear, from her lips and onto her chin.

"Oh my goodness," Lydia said, and Martha, for the first time, turned around.

As she did, the woman took a napkin, held it to her mouth, and left. They watched her though the glass door, and through the windows, as she walked across the parking lot, still holding the napkin to her lips, and got into the passenger side of the car where the man who had done this to her was sitting behind the steering wheel with the engine running, waiting on her.

WHILE THE EVENTS at the restaurant were happening, Monroe was home, alone, sitting at the dining room table with an old-style adding machine in front of him.

He was calculating how much money he had, and how much he would make for overtime, and how much he would need if he actually quit his job. He also had an atlas, and the atlas was turned to pages in the western part of the states. He had never lived out West before.

Lydia was gone. It had been hell to get rid of her. But she was gone. Some people took a hint right away. Some never took it. He'd been forced to get mean with her, to make her leave. No one liked to be mean to another person, but sometimes it was necessary.

He made tea. Lydia bought many kinds of tea. The tea was in boxes and tins on the shelf beside the stove. She forgot to take the tea when she left. He chose a flavor, and poured the water over the tea bag, and returned to the table.

The table and the chairs and even the teapot in which he boiled the water belonged to the people who owned the house. The adding machine was his. The television, and the chair upstairs by the window, and the bed that Lydia had hoped would crash apart so that he might see what he'd done to her belonged to the house.

He had only his clothes. The clothes he had were all bought within the past few years. Everything else he had ever had burned up in Katy's fire, and now he was left with only a few boxes and suitcases, and he could throw those in the back of his car, and be gone in an hour.

MARTHA COULD NOT OPEN the door. It had been difficult to unlock since they moved in. The night she and Lydia had gone to dinner, she fought the lock for what seemed like hours before it released. It was not what they'd seen that night that caused the trouble. It was more than that.

It was the irreducible arrhythmia of her heart, fluttering, not from joy, but from the effort of belief, as if she were trying to fly her iron lung toward an escadrille that soared ahead of her, a blinding vision of happiness and peace and communion, she could not catch.

This burdened flight crashed into the lock each day. It was not entirely her fault. The lock was a cheap one. The cheaper the lock, the less easily the mechanism turned. The worst ones lacked the fluidity of the better ones, and their tumblers and cogs scraped and dragged, and were poorly aligned. Some people fought these locks, and bruised their fingers, tiny bones, easily broken.

The lock would not be fought. It would not operate under duress. If forced, it froze. It would only operate if you suspended the key within its contours, and then, turned as slowly as possible.

The lock was a test you had to pass before you could enter. It was also a sign. It was a mandate for you to stop and consider whether this was what you should be doing, entering this building, and it was a pause in which you were to contemplate what would happen once you entered.

If you were angry, or distraught, or out of control, for any reason, you could not enter. The lock simply would not release.

The lock was a version of Chinese handcuffs, whereby you stuck your fingers into the woven tubes, which then, through your own struggles, tightened up so that you tied yourself to yourself in such a way that you could only be freed after you relaxed and reflected on how it came to be, that you had done this to yourself.

In the door above the lock, at eye level, was a magnifying peephole. It reversed the magnification, though, so that Earl, inside, and watching Martha struggle with the lock, saw her as if she were a toy, a doll, with a sad, little body and an enormous head the size of a balloon.

LYDIA PHONED HER mother. It was two A.M.

"I can't sleep," she said.

"I never sleep," her mother said. "That's why I told you to call anytime."

"I'm getting tired of being wrong. I'm getting so tired of making mistakes, and I know, you told me. You told me and I didn't listen, but how could I know I was wrong? How? He was a doctor. He was a good man. He is a good man. Just not with me, though, and how could I know that, pray tell me, before I got involved with him? How?"

"You couldn't I guess, but forget about it. It's just life."

"I know. Just life. It happens to everyone. To everything. I saw something this afternoon that made me feel so sad."

"What was it?" her mother asked.

"It was a bird that was flying against my window, and I sat there and watched it smack into the glass, and then fall backwards, and then kind of stand up and scratch its face with its little claws, its little feet, and then it would fly off and make a circle and then hover back in front of the window and smack into it again, and then again, and I sat there, watching it, until finally, one time, it hit the window and fell onto the grass and didn't get up."

"It knocked its brains out."

"I guess it did, because I brought it inside, and it was still alive. You can't feel the heart of a bird beating, not easily, because it's so small, just this tiny, frail thing, but I held the bird to my cheek, and I could feel something, and I cupped it in my hands, and tried to keep it warm, but it died. It just died."

"It wasn't your fault," her mother said.

"I thought, after it died, that this was the first time I had ever been with anything that actually died. I mean, was actually there, as the life went out of it, as it took its last breath, at the last moment, you know, and I wondered if there was something about the way people die nowadays, and animals die, you know, put to sleep, and all, that is not supposed to be, because I was thinking, that if you were there when life departed, if you were there at the moment when life left the little creature, or the person, then you would be given something, in the dying, and I don't know what, but you would be given something, like some help in understanding life, why and what it is that life is all about, something, though. You would be there, and you would then know something you didn't know before."

"Death is no fun to be around," her mother said.

"You might be able to understand a little more about why in heaven's name you do the things you do, and think the things you think, and act the way you act. I don't know, Mother. It's just that I got upset at myself for just sitting there, watching that bird beat itself to death, and not doing anything about it."

"I believe you need to go on that cruise with me. You're beginning to sound like your father when he drank."

"How was that? You've never told me that before. What did he do?"

"Cry. Lord, would he cry. Just weep and weep like a baby, and go on and on about his life, and all the things he'd done wrong. Why, that's just the way it goes, I'd tell him. But he never could get over things. He never could. They stayed with him, and stayed with him, and he had to leave, I think, to get away from all that he couldn't forget. I think that's why he left."

"You think so?"

"I know he loved us. All of us. But he couldn't control himself, and he kept getting into trouble, couldn't hold a job, couldn't control his temper, couldn't stay steady. You should have heard him when he was drunk. He was the most up and down man, I do believe, ever existed."

"I wish you'd told me all this earlier."

"It doesn't do any good to know it. People are what they are. That's about it."

"I'm not so sure."

"It doesn't matter, as far as I've seen, what people tell you. You are what you are, and that's about it."

MARTHA SHUT THE door to her bedroom. Earl and the three men in the other room were playing cards, drinking, and had ordered a pizza. There was no lock on her door, but this was probably for the best, because if there had been, it would likely not work, or would jam just as you wanted to release it, thereby trapping you in. Some people thought a chair propped under the knob, and wedged against the floor, would secure a door. This was not true.

Martha turned on the radio. She propped her feet on some pillows, and lay flat on the bed. The bed consisted of a box spring with legs screwed into each corner and a mattress on top of that. There was no headboard and nothing at the foot. One of the legs had been missing since she hauled it over, and Earl had stacked up two bricks to level it.

A brick is approximately two inches tall, by four inches wide, by eight inches long. Because they only had two bricks, and because they needed to achieve six inches in height to match the three remaining legs, they put one brick flat and the other one on edge. This made the bed wobbly.

Because the bed was wobbly, Earl tried to be careful with Martha, and when he finished, and left her there, he fell dead drunk asleep in the spare bedroom, and never even knew that his three friends had not only knocked the bed off the bricks, so that they had to grip the edge of the mattress above them while they enjoyed Martha, but that they had broken off the other leg on that same side, as well.

It was a bad night for Martha, because the boys got confused with the idea of a woman who would do anything, and they beat her and took her out on the balcony, hung her over the edge, and tied her, by her hair, to one of the railings, so that she took the form, in the night, in the glow of the streetlights, of an omen, took the form of an ancient human sacrifice, a lesson that this is what awaited those who violated the beliefs of the people.

These men had never studied anthropology. They wouldn't know an anthropologist from an archaeopteryx, but they repeated the punishment for sensuality, for desire, for wantonness from times past. These three men, like the priests or elders of old, knew they had to sacrifice this woman.

There was historical precedent for it. Because of this, these particular men could not be blamed. Maybe it was in their genes. Maybe deep down it was.

Wantonness in women would always be punished.

The Rwani tribe used to hang their women upside down from a tower for three days. The Mogids, a nomadic people in what used to be known as Persia, used to punish the women who challenged established beliefs and authority by hanging them by their hair over the side of a camel and taking the camel far into the wilderness, where the miscreant, the infidel, would have time to think about what she'd done.

32

THERE WAS GRACE AND style to the way Martha hung in the air, as if it were a circus act itself, and one could admire a woman who could hang like that, so quietly, so still, waiting to be released.

Earl had known nothing about it. He found her the next morning. He took her to the hospital.

"I'm sorry," he said.

After something like this, you could say you were sorry. The right kind of woman had been trained since childhood to believe she was no good, and that everything was her fault, all the bad, all the trouble. These women often made terrific lovers, and could take all kinds of abuse, give their hearts to you in bed, and out, and then you could do anything you wanted to them.

Sometimes, you could beat them, and not even say you were sorry, and they still assumed you loved them. They'd been so well trained you could even get away with that.

"I'm sorry," he said.

You could make these women do anything. They

worked all week, gave you their paychecks, cooked, cleaned, took a fist in the mouth, or the back, and then picked themselves off the floor, maybe quietly asked that you not, please, do that again, and returned to work, right where they'd left off.

It was a fabulous arrangement, and most of the fellows who ended up with these women could find one in a crowd of 50,000. They could pick them out, and woo them, and have them pregnant, holding down two jobs, sleeping with their friends, and bearing injuries reported to have occurred while falling down the stairs or running into doors that opened into their faces. These gals could take it.

"I'm sorry," he said.

A social worker was sent to the apartment, along with the police. It appeared to be a case of domestic violence.

It was not quite that simple, however, because now, everyone had heard about the woman up north who had broken her own neck while having sex.

Suppose, and a good lawyer would always suppose all there was to suppose, suppose Martha, from the looks of the apartment, had run around the room, bashing into the walls and smashing her fists through the partitions.

Suppose she had smashed her head into the door, and ripped the hinges loose, damaged the locks, all of this in a fit of sexual frustration and frenzy.

Once an idea such as this had been introduced, it became easier to accept, and thus, it was not entirely without probability that Martha had done this to herself, in a long night of frustration and rage.

The evening had begun pleasantly. Earl and a few of the boys were playing cards. Martha returned from an evening out. Seeing all those men, she lost control.

As the evening progressed, she became more and more aroused. She savagely attacked the men, who fled in fear and horror.

After the men left, Earl passed out from his exertions with her. It had not been enough. She then ran through the rooms, bashing holes in the walls. There. Look. There were the holes. Everywhere. In every room. She had rushed into the kitchen, and torn the cabinets loose, and broken the legs off the furniture.

She mounted the doorknobs, kicked the chairs, and turned over the tables and threw herself upon the floor. It had gone on and on. She ripped her clothes off. She bit her own lips. She threw herself into the air and off the balcony.

The lawyers could point to all the precedents, including the woman who was supposedly jogging through the park after work one evening, but who actually was running in a hellish frenzy of swollen desire, and threw herself into a crowd of little boys.

The boys had actually been the victims, as this woman, and Martha, and others elsewhere, suddenly pulled their hair, and tore off their clothes, broke their own necks, and then, in shame and repentance, hung themselves off balconies.

33

RONNIE GOT IN MONROE'S bed. The house was dark. The light from the front porch shone through the window. The window had white curtains, bordered in lace. The bed had a carved, walnut headboard, and a smaller one, with smaller posts, at the foot.

Monroe was at the hospital, and Ronnie took off her clothes and eased into the bed, and hugged his pillow, and rubbed herself all over with his sheets, and kissed the pillow, and made it kiss her all over, and she giggled and laughed and tossed around, pretending and playing and having fun.

She then gathered up her clothes, and carried them into the kitchen. She opened the refrigerator. It was nearly empty. She had a craving for a Coke, a real Coke in a small old-fashioned bottle. All the ones he kept for her were empty, and the empty bottles were in a carton on top of the refrigerator.

She dressed, and ran out the back door, and down the dark street. The street was empty. The patrol would have passed by that time. She ran her route, through the ravine, across a few backyards, barking dogs, one fence to jump, and through the back lot of the all-night convenience store.

"So, you have returned," the Pakistani woman clerk said when she saw Ronnie. "I have not seen you in a long time."

"I've been busy," she said. "I got me a boyfriend."

"Then that is why you smile like you do, like you cannot stop."

"You got it. I love this guy. I've been looking for a cowpoke like him forever. Now I got him."

"That sounds nice."

"I even got me some new britches to wear. He picked them out. He bought them for me. He likes to buy me things."

"Britches?"

"That's just cowpoke talk for pants. Slacks. You know. Sometimes he likes me in a dress, sometimes in pants. I let him pick the stuff out."

An old ambulance, without the lights on the roof, stopped in front of the store. The vehicle was covered with slogans and crude paintings of men and women, and monkeys hanging from trees, scenes from the Bible, and taking up the entire rear door, where the dead or victims would have been loaded, a detailed drawing of Armageddon, titled as such.

"Oh, no," the clerk said. "Him again."

Beside the man who'd been driving, sat a girl with blonde hair. The hair was dirty and uncombed. When the man slammed the door on his side, the girl fell over against her door. Ronnie passed the man, on his way in, on her way out, and read the sayings, and looked at the pictures.

After she finished, she leaned against the front of the store. The man came out with a bag in one hand and his keys in the other. He unlocked his door, and removed a candy bar from the bag and set it on the girl's lap. Then he said something to her, and began to eat and drink what he'd bought, himself.

When he finished, he dragged the woman from the seat, and laid her on a mattress behind him. Ronnie got as close as she dared and peered in the windshield, and saw the girl's top was bare, and that her legs had broken off when she'd been pulled from the front to the mattress, and Ronnie realized she was a mannequin.

Oh lord, she thought. It's not a real woman.

"Did you see that?" she asked the clerk. "Did you see what that fellow was riding around with?"

"Yes. He always has her with him."

"It was an artificial woman."

"The man gives me the creeps."

"I've got to tell Monroe about this," Ronnie said, and ran out the door. "He's going to love it."

ANY TRAUMA TO THE head was dangerous. There could be blood clots. A violent blow to the head could make the brain itself slosh around inside the skull. If this happens, and bleeding results, the person becomes lethargic. Sometimes people who get beaten were lethargic to begin with, so this might not be a change.

If the trauma to the head is severe, and directly impacts the brain itself, the brain cells can tear. This causes a person to become unconscious, and brain cells may die, and never regenerate, making the person what is commonly known as punch-drunk. A punch-drunk woman would be a sight indeed.

An unconscious person can regain consciousness immediately, as with the case of a boxer who is flattened and gets up before the count of ten. Often, it's longer, and the longer one is out, the more serious it is.

A person usually has trouble talking after a severe beating, and this is called dysphasia, and sometimes trouble swallowing, which is called dysphagia. When the whites of the eyes turn red, it may be a sign of subconjunctival hemorrhage.

Subconjunctival hemorrhage is bad, but if you've been crying and crying a long, long time, your eyes also get red. If you've been drinking beer all day and were welled up with rage and hatred, your eyes turn red, also, red being the color of rage, distress, and passion.

Though it was never shown in the old movies, when a person is scalped, or the hair is partially torn from the scalp, there's a lot of blood. The scalp is a rich blood supply area, and beneath it is a layer called the galea aponeurotica. This layer might, or might not, hold, if someone were hung by her hair.

The jawbone is another matter. It is usually not broken in a fight or a mild beating. It often fractures, but rarely actually breaks. When the jawbone breaks, it usually breaks near the joint, near the condyle or the ramus, near the hinge, as if the person had her mouth open and was trying to say something when she was hit, or had her mouth open wide, and was screaming, for instance, when the blow landed.

Martha's head was far beyond normal size. She looked like the pumpkin-head boy from the Oz books. She looked like an angry girl, who'd said, I'll hold my breath until I die, until I explode, and had. She looked like a comical clay figure, made by a child, that's all head, and below that, a crooked, undersized torso, with tiny arms and legs attached at the wrong places, the wrong angles, and the mouth and nose pinched into the clay out of line. She looked like one of those frightful inflated figures that hover above parades, a celebration, in this instance, of despair and trouble and terminal confusion.

Monroe did not recognize Martha until he saw her

name on the chart, and met Earl, who was standing beside her.

"Well, I reckon the boys got a little carried away," he said, trying to explain to Monroe what happened.

"You reckon?" Monroe asked. "You reckon this is what's called, getting a little carried away?"

"I do believe it started out in fun," Earl said. "I mean to say, the boys didn't start out meaning no harm."

"I hold you responsible for this," Monroe told him.

"It wasn't my fault," he said. "I was passed out."

"I expect the courts'll decide whose fault it was."

"Yes sir."

"Get out of my sight now, Earl. I'm getting a little tired of people like you. If you don't like a woman, there are better ways to get rid of them than beat them up. You hear me?"

"I didn't beat her up."

"I've got my work to do," Monroe told him, and started walking away. "Besides, I've got to call Lydia and tell her about this."

"Yes sir."

"I hate this job," he said, and left Earl standing beside the policeman who was ready to take down his account of the events of the night.

FOUR DAYS LATER, MONROE had not told Ronnie
about what happened to Martha, and had not told her
that he had seen and talked to Lydia, the first time in
many months, that night, after he called her to let
her know Martha would survive, would recover, but
would need her help.

He had not told Ronnie because there was no
reason to upset her about such things, or to ask her
to understand such things, and there was no reason
to become involved in them any further, because he
and Ronnie would soon be leaving town.

"Will we see Roy?" Ronnie asked.

Life does continue. People must learn from their
mistakes. Excess and passion have their limits. These
simple truths had been known forever.

"We might see old Roy," Monroe said.

It was wonderful to stop work at the hospital, and
to start life anew with Ronnie. It was a delight to be
with her. It was such a relief to find the right person.
Who would have imagined, with all the excitement
these days about tall women, about fast-moving

women, about fearless women, about powerful women
with sculpted muscles and runner's legs, and faces that
dared anyone to stop them, that it would turn out to
be an eighteen-year-old girl, for whom the world was
a joyous puzzle with pieces missing, who would have
guessed that this would be what the fellows were really
looking for, hoping for, longing for.

"I hope we do," she said. "I love Roy."

This woman warrior thing sounded like a good
idea at first. It seemed it would be fun. The boys were
excited, initially, and agreed to it. Later, it was not
much fun. It appears now most of them wanted the
woman as child, that it was Ronnie, after all, and not
the warriors.

"He is still alive," Monroe said, referring to Roy.

It was horrifying to think of a woman breaking
her own neck making love, or throwing herself into a
crowd of little boys, or letting her husband turn her
into the high priestess of a thousand men. It seemed
impossible to be true. It seemed as if none of it could
actually have happened.

It seemed like something that later would be found
to have been hysteria and rumors, in the same way
that the reports of chastity leagues turned out to
be untrue. Maybe it began after the Krazy Glue episode.

"How about Dale?" Ronnie asked. "Isn't she still
alive?"

That people would throw themselves into walls,
and break off doorknobs, and hang off balconies and
let educated men in fine suits beat their daughters to
death while they read, or watched TV, or went numb,
in the next room, could not be true.

"Dale's alive. I saw her and Roy on 'Entertainment
Tonight' just a few days ago," Monroe said. He loved

that show. It was a happy show, and he watched it every night.

The warrior thing had scared some of the boys pretty bad. Even the ones who liked it at first, and were thrilled by what these new women would do, and, in their excitement, loaned them out to their best friends, even they eventually became confused and remorseful, and tried to stop it.

"Good," Ronnie said. "I want to meet her, too."

Some of the fellows went too far. The vision of the Victorian figurine, in long skirts, who demurely looked away, who knew how to avert her eyes, who was startled by what had been asked of her, the vision of that, existing at the same time as the high priestess of a thousand men, and the woman jogging through the park, when she, according to the old beliefs, should have been home looking startled, being quiet, blushing, and waiting to be told what to do next, the vision of all that happening at once, was too confusing.

"I want to be wearing the same outfit she wore in the movies when I meet her," Ronnie said.

"Old Gabby Hayes is dead, though."

"He was funny. I loved old Gabby. He was always so grouchy. He made me laugh."

"I loved him, too," Monroe said. "He makes me laugh, as well."

"He makes you smile, too, doesn't he," she said, and poked him in his dimples, which made him smile all the more.

"He makes me smile, you make me smile, and I'm afraid I'm going to be a smiling fool from now on," he said.

"A gall-durned smiling fool," she said, and kissed him.

They sat on the floor. In front of them was an

atlas. They traced the cities and towns along the routes as they planned their trip.

"Listen, sweetheart," he said. "The first night, let's stay here, right here just the other side of the mountains."

"Where?"

"In the town of, let me see," he said and searched for one at the approximate distance they might comfortably travel in one day. "Right here in the town of Faraway, Tennessee."

"Anywhere," she said. "I'll stay anywhere, Faraway, or anywhere else, as long as it's with you."

That was the kind of statement that was nice to hear. It was the kind of thing women used to say, long ago. They stopped saying it. Now, it was being said again.

"This is going to be so wonderful," he said. "So fabulous. So simply and utterly fabulous. I can't wait. I really and truly can't. I haven't felt this good, in so long, I can't even remember when it was."

"Me, too."

"I never have to step foot in that hospital again. I never have to see anyone I don't want to again. I feel great. I just feel bonkers, great. Spectacular, even. No more work, no more sad, desperate Lydia. No more nothing, but you and me, my little desert rose."

"You and me," she repeated.

"Right."

"Right."

"Repeat it all you want," he said. "It feels good."

Monroe put the atlas to one side. It belonged to the family who owned the house. If he took it on the trip, the family might miss it. Then again, they might not.

He left the room to get a current road map from

his car, and when he returned, Ronnie flew against him, across the room, airborne, and into his arms, as if he'd been away for years.

"Why didn't you like her, anyway?" she asked.

"Who? Lydia?"

"Yes."

"I don't know. Everything. All kinds of things. It's too complicated, honestly, to go into. Just say, for instance, she was too tall. Just leave it at that. Just pretend that was the reason."

"You don't like tall girls?"

"I thought I did. I guess I don't."

"How about me?" she asked.

"You are perfect."

"Really?"

"Yes."

"And you like me?"

"Yes. More than anyone. More than anything."

"And you love me?"

"Forever, sweetheart, my little prairie princess. Forever."

"Good," she said. "Now, where's the next place we'll stay?"

"I do believe we can make it, by the second day, into Arkansas."

"That's where our maid's from."

"I assumed that," he said, and poked her in her own dimples as she smiled, peering closely into his own smiling face. "Will she miss you?" he asked.

"She might. She probably will."

"Send her a postcard."

"Okay. I'll do that. A funny one."

"What's the matter?" he asked, as her smile faded.

"I was thinking of Daddy. And Mother, even. I'm probably going to miss them. For a while I thought I would only miss Daddy, but I think I might miss the old bear herself."

"You might."

"Nevertheless," she said, remembering one of the first words they'd used together, "nevertheless, I'll be glad it's over."

"You're safe now."

"I know."

"You're loved now."

"I know. I know it, baby."

"I'll take good care of you."

"I know you will, but I just wish there was some way to tell them before we actually leave."

"It's better this way. You'll see. Everything will be fine."

"More than fine. The finest. The absolute finest."

They kissed again. They kissed all day long. They kissed hundreds of times. They couldn't stop. It was that good.

"This trip is going to be the nibs. Just the absolute nibs," he said. "It's going to be fab-u-lo-so," he said, sounding like Lydia in his unrestrained enthusiasm. "It really is, my little gal."

"That's what I am," she said, and hugged him. "Just your little gal."

"Next stop, after Faraway, then, how about," he said, and traced his finger along the map, "how about Buena Vista, Arkansas?"

"Sounds just right. And where'll we stay?"

"In a motel, darling. Where else?"

"I know. Just as long as it has a bed, right?"

"Sure. That'll be all we need."

"I'm getting wild thinking about it. I swear, I feel like doing it all the time," she said.

"I know, sweetheart. It's that old hormone they

call the love hormone, oxytocin. When it fires off, there's nothing like it."

"I don't know what it is, and don't care what it is, but I sure do love it. I could do it right now. I swear I could."

"Uh huh."

"And to hell with the oxytocin. It's you that does it to me. You, sweet man. Just you."

Their destination was California. They were traveling to Victorville, which was south of Barstow, and just north of San Bernardino. Victorville was the location of the Roy Rogers and Dale Evans Museum, and Roy and Dale lived on a ranch nearby.

"Show me Victorville," she said.

"There."

"Trigger's inside, you know."

"I read that."

"And Buttermilk, and Bullet. All stuffed."

"Weird," he said.

"I know, but neat, also. Nellybelle is there, as well."

"I wonder if old Gabby is there, stuffed," he asked.

"No, you durned fool," she said, imitating Gabby's irritable manner. "He ain't a one for that kind of dad-blamed nonsense."

"I guess not."

"You know what else I want to do?"

"What?"

"I want us to walk in a bar, somewhere out West, and knock open those swinging doors, and walk up to the bar, and say, give me a sasparilly. I always wanted a sasparilly."

"We can do that," he said.

"You're smiling again," she said. "You're staring off into space, and smiling."

"Of course I am."

"Can I ask you something?"

"You can ask me anything," he said. "Anything at all."

"You promise you won't mind?"

"I promise."

"You know, the last time, when we did it, the way you had me be still?"

"Yes."

"Is that the way I have to do it every time?"

"I guess not. Didn't you like it?"

"Oh, yes. Oh, yes, yes, yes. I did. I did. I really did. But it's not easy to be still like that. It's not easy at all."

"It was just an idea. Something I'd been thinking about."

"But is that the way you want me to do it, from now on?"

"No. But it *is* the way people used to do it."

"Is that the way Lydia was?"

"No. She was not that way. Not at all."

"How about Katy?"

"I can't remember."

"I can understand them not being that way," Ronnie said. "It's not easy to be still. Not easy at all. But I'll do it, if that's what you want. I'll be any way you want me to be."

"I know you will, sweet girl. That's why I love you so much."

They returned the atlas to the shelf. Monroe's new car was air conditioned. They could go anywhere. Once you found the right person, you could do anything. The right girl made a fellow like Monroe, who'd met a few of these newfangled women, mighty happy, buckaroos, it sure enough did.

KATY WOMEN

CHAPTER

36

A FEW WEEKS AGO, I saw Monroe at the mall. He was across the tangle of fountains and plants, and he was with a woman who held his arm.

I had not seen him in years. When I left him, almost six years ago, after deciding I would have to leave or die, I never heard from him again, except that one visit to the hospital. I never received a phone call, never got a letter, nor did I ever mail the ones I, myself, wrote to him, waiting, always waiting, for him to act first.

I spent a year away from everyone. My brother came to see me once, an emissary from the family, but he kept my confidence, and they never knew how truly awful I really felt. I moved to my deceased uncle's house in a remote section of the Blue Ridge Mountains. It was a house I had visited as a child, and now it was empty, waiting for me.

I thought about all that had happened. I thought, now Katy, you learned so much in school. You did. You can remember that. You went to school, and studied the wisdom and inspiration and vision of others, of great thinkers, and enlightened men and women, and all that you learned made sense to you, and you became enamored by this idea of knowledge, the fearlessness of knowing all there was to know, and then, going beyond.

I remembered that, but then I met Monroe, and almost everything I knew started to leave me, as if all that I had learned failed when I needed it most, until, much later, I felt as empty as he seemed to want me to be, and as homeless without him, as an addict on the street.

Moving into Uncle Walt's house, though, was perfect. He'd been a radical at Columbia when he and six of his friends, in 1923, dropped out to start a crafts commune in the North Carolina mountains. It did not succeed, according to family lore, and he went on his own, wrote for left-wing magazines, and then lived on the family money, until he died.

When he built this house, the local people told him, you can't build there. You cannot build that close to the river. People who try that will be killed. People who build that close, won't live long. The house will be swept away. You can't do it, they told him. Nobody can build there.

So the house stood, high on piers, above the rage of the river, above the doubt of the local people, above the concerns of the world below, and I came here to learn about solitude, and to remember what it was, what it had been, that I had known and seen, before I went blind and crazy, and began to burn away, a fire metaphor that once became too real, and I don't want to think about it, even now.

My parents knew something was wrong with my marriage. My brother, whom I love so much, and who is in the peace corps, still in the peace corps, still thinking he can change the world, though he comes back now and again and chases his old girlfriends and wastes himself for a few weeks each year, knew something was wrong, but I lied to them. I lied to myself. I did not know it was a lie.

Are you all right? they'd ask. You don't seem all right. You don't seem yourself. Is it money? they'd ask. No, it was not money. There's always been plenty of money. My grandfather had been a famous surgeon, and my father was a doctor, a GP, but loaded up with all the rich patients in town, so that the specialists leapt into the air whenever they received a phone call from him, and so there'd always been plenty of money, and even I, myself, had my own money, along with my brother, from my grandmother's trust fund, which paid me enough, year after year, and still does, to do almost anything I want.

So, no, I'd say. It's not money. We have plenty. We have plenty of that, but my mother would look at me and ask, what is it, then? Tell me. Tell me so I can do something about it. Tell me, so at least I can know what it is. Because, she'd say, you don't seem happy.

Oh, yes, I would say. I am happy. I am, I am, I am.

So after I left Monroe, I moved to Uncle Walt's house, and I sat on the porch, not only overlooking the river, but actually over the river, a cantilevered porch that would give an engineer a heart attack, but there I sat, day after day, smoking and thinking, and then smoking and thinking some more, watching the river, and feeling its turbulence.

The way I felt, still and quiet, and yet aroused, reminded me of the first time I became aware of such diffuse and contradictory feelings.

My brother had volunteered me to be the female assistant in his best friend's one-time magic show. I was fourteen. We rehearsed. The magic boy touched me, and moved my legs where he wanted them, and my arms where he wanted them, and he touched my face to make me look the way he wanted, and he spread out my hair beside me, the way he wanted it to be, and I had chills all over from his touch, and I abandoned myself to him.

The unexpected arousal of it all caught me by surprise, and I still wonder, to this day, why it felt so good, and why, at times, when everything is going well, and one finds oneself with the right man, it still does.

But that was a long, long time ago, and I saw Monroe yesterday, and followed him. He and his sweetheart went into a Chick-Fil-A, of all things. We *never* ate in places like that. *Never.* She fed him morsels of little brown nuggets, which she dipped into one of three sauces, in plastic cups, between them, and she licked her fingers, and swooned toward him, as if she were tasting him, and I thought, who is this man, being fed by a strange-looking, hard-faced woman, who appears to have seen too much of life, and all that she'd seen had been imprinted on her face, a woman, wearing, of all things, an ankle bracelet, with short shorts and high heels, and a tight, knit top, and I watched them, and then I left, but only after deciding I would call him, and talk to him, and tell him everything I always wanted to tell him, and find out about his life, and let him know why I am in town.

37

I GREW UP LOVING men because, I suppose, the men in my childhood loved me so much. My grandfather, the famous surgeon, used to bring my brother and me comic books. He'd give them to us privately, in the back of the house. I thought it was because he wanted to show he'd done something special for us, but my mother later told me my grandmother disapproved of comic books, and the famous old man had to sneak them in to us.

So, my grandfather loved me, and treated me as if I were the love of his life, and Daddy was the same way. When Monroe and I were about to marry, Daddy had a long talk with him. Monroe told me about it that night. My father said, I want to tell you about Katy. She's a strong girl, and she's a smart girl, but she also has deep feelings. Deep, deep feelings, he said.

He knew that, because he was the same way. We used to watch old movies together on TV, late at night, after everyone had gone to bed, and we'd both cry in the sad parts, my father, the son of the renowned surgeon, and a god-like physician himself to his patients, would sit up late with me and cry at sad movies, and hold me against his shoulder.

But he told Monroe what he thought about me, and he said, Monroe, she's in love with you. Remember that. She's not been in love with any other fellow in her life, and she's giving you something. She's giving you the gift of her love, and most men your age don't understand that, and they won't understand it, until it's too late.

So, later that night, Monroe told me what Daddy had said, and I thought it so sweet, and I thought it just like him to say it, to think it, to do it, to tell this man I was going to marry, how much he, himself, loved me, because that is what he was saying. Looking back, I wonder what a fool, what an innocent, trusting little girl I must have been, and how I must have made that depressingly common mistake of assuming my husband would be like my father.

Did I do that? Did I do that to myself, after knowing it would not be true, could not be true? I did, and so now, I believe that knowledge and learning have very little effect on what you actually do, on how you actually live, and that it's something else, something heavenly, or hellish, that occurs, that you actually embrace, both probably, a little of both.

Page, my best friend for all times, always says to me, Katy, just don't think too much. Just quit thinking all the time. And I say, well Page, what would we be if we didn't think. Happy, she says.

People change, though. Monroe was, in a way, if you were in love with him, somewhat like my father, except he was from a broken family, and a working-class family, but had set his sights high, and had made it, and I had met him while I was an undergraduate and he was in medical school, and he was, at the time, the best man I had ever met, the kindest, sweetest, most intelligent, most idealistic, most fun man I had ever met.

I had been wild in college. I'd been wild because I always felt different from everyone else, and the only way I knew how to express it was by being wild, mostly with men, mostly with terminal-case, cold-hearted men you would never make the mistake of marrying, and one day a friend overheard one of these jerks talking to Monroe.

I hear you went out with Katy Trent last night, the guy said. You must have had some fun, because she's been around, and she knows what she's doing. She's been with every man in town.

Well, this was not true. But anyway, I was told Monroe said nothing for a while, and then, in a forceful and low and deliberate way, he told this guy, well, if that's so, then there must be a lot of very happy men in town, because Katy certainly makes me happy. And then he walked away.

I loved him when I heard that. I loved him for sticking up for me, and for putting that jerk in his place. That was the man I married. I made him happy. Think of the richness in being able to make someone happy. And he understood me. Then we got married, and then he dropped out of medical school for a few years, because the war was going on, and everyone hated Dow Chemical and all that, and we moved to Maine, to a farm a relative owned but never lived there, and I had an old car that said, on a sticker on the bumper, INNER PEACE IS WORLD PEACE, and I believed it. I believed that, and I believed everything else I wanted to believe, and I did so as long as I could.

MONROE WAS IN THE phone book. I looked it up, and there was his name, his address, and his phone number. Why did I think he would have an unlisted number?

I did not have a phone the year I lived in the mountains. I was not available. To get to me, you had to really want to. To find me, you had to want to, with all your heart.

The road to Uncle Walt's house was actually an old rail bed. Loggers built these roads before the turn of the century to haul down the timber. From my house, I could see the remains of the town's glory, and even the old, three-story hotel, which had fallen in on itself, and I could dream about the simple and uncomplicated lives of the men and women who stayed there, dream about it, because I'm not sure it was so.

The road, though, curved around the mountains for twenty miles, and it took more than an hour to drive it. On one side was always the sheer face of the mountain, of the cut made into it years earlier to establish the level ground.

On the other side, always, was the drop-off of the ravine below, and, at the bottom of the ravine, the river.

Finding the old town, and my uncle's house, and driving this road was a journey, a mythological journey, and one was changed by the trip, by the concentration and the danger of the expedition itself. Once there, you did not want to go back, unless you had to.

I did go back, for Christmas. I did that. I always spend Christmas with my family, and my brother always comes home from Honduras or Botswana, or wherever he is, because Christmas in my family is holy and sacred, in every possible way, and, of course, happy and fun at the same time. Everyone has some little thing he or she always does, always says, always wears, always acts out, and it's impossible to convey to anyone how goofy we all get, and how endlessly funny, to us, the rituals of the family Christmas are.

I tried to give my family, and our Christmas, to Monroe. I tried. He did not have a family in the sense I did, and I let him in, and we welcomed him. For a while, he seemed to understand us, and to know, and feel the richness of our life, that we always had each other, no matter what, and now, he was a part of that, and he would always have us, but I guess it did not take.

In the clarity and wisdom of retrospect, that was one of my naive attractions to him. I had been given so much. I had been given a life so full and so rich, and he seemed to need that, to need all the things I had, that had been given to me, so I thought, well, sure, I can give anything to him, because there is plenty.

So I married him, and began to give, and I gave so much, I forgot about myself. It took me forever to realize what I was doing and to understand that wanting things for myself was all right.

So I left Monroe, and moved to Uncle Walt's, and I thought I'd brought enough with me to last, but after the first week, I had a list of things I needed, hardware stuff, like those round, screw-in fuses that blow all the time, and I had a craving for chocolate, so I drove to the larger town, twenty miles below, to get my supplies.

I think now I went back because I needed to be with people again. I had rendered myself into isolation too quickly, and I was afraid, afraid of what I'd done in leaving my marriage, not sure it was right, and afraid, honestly, of being alone, when I had never been. I did not sleep well, and I paced back and forth all day, sometimes, pretending to be doing something, but mostly just pacing, sitting, getting up, walking outside, back in, out to the porch, drinking a little wine, and smoking, for the first few months, about twenty-four hours a day.

But I went to town, and while I was gone, it began to rain. It rained hard. I had to stop the car. I could not see where I was going. It took hours to get down the mountain. I never met another car on the way down. Some people have better sense than others, and these old hill folks know when to stay indoors.

I saw a few of them as I passed. They watched me from windows, from porches, from inside barns, or sheds, and, knowing them as I do now, they remembered my car from a week earlier, and would begin to record, in their minds, the history of my life up there, and when they first saw me, and what they thought, and how it all evolved, and they'd slowly connect what they knew about me with what they'd known about my uncle, and they would contemplate me, and my year up there, in much the same way I would contemplate and reflect on them, and myself, and would be learning about them, and about this Katy-girl-in-hiding, but they would not bother me, and they would not intrude on me, and I would leave them be, until the time was right.

But it rained so hard, and for so long, that when I finally got to town, I waited in my car for the water in the streets to subside, and then I got out, and I shopped, and heard the people talking about how high the rivers would be, because the hill folk keep up with things like rain and floods, having been washed away too many times to ignore them.

I did not know about the power of such things then, or only knew in the way a child knows about thunder and lightning, or only in the way one intellectualizes the elements. After I drove home, exhausted and wired at the same time, I unpacked my supplies, and ate my second chocolate bar, and I lay on the bed, trying to be quiet, and relax.

I could hear the river roaring like I'd never heard it. About the same time I realized the river was making so much noise, I began to tremble.

I tried to think of things that would make me feel better, and not so frightened, and not so alone, and not so upset with myself for making such a mess of my life, but I could not stop trembling, and it scared me, and I thought, I might not make it up here. I might not. I might have to go back. I might even die. I might actually die.

I could not breathe. I felt too scared, and too full of the shakes, but then the rain slacked off, and then the sun came out, and I went outside, and lay on the ground. I felt awful. I felt desperate and confused, and

I rubbed my face in the ground, hard, as hard as I could bear it, and then, even harder.

I hurt myself, because he had hurt me so badly. I lay against the earth, and rocked my head back and forth, with my face in the grass, so that I hurt as much as I could make myself hurt, and then, finally, I stopped.

I rolled onto my back. I spit dirt from my mouth, and wiped away the mud, and the tears, and I felt so much better, but I was still trembling. Then, I realized that it had not only been me that was trembling, but the earth itself, from the force of the river, swollen, and rushing against its banks with such power, that the earth itself, had begun to tremble.

Someone could have probably told me about this, but I had to learn it for myself. When it rains hard, very hard, the river rises. It forces itself against its banks. The earth along the banks begins to tremble. It happens every time.

Later, during that year, I would welcome the wildness of the river, and would lie in bed, half asleep, and trembling, and loving every single, exhilarating, glorious minute of it. But that was later. A long way off. At that time, a long, long way off.

I'M GOING TO DRIVE to Monroe's house soon. I've already talked to Thomas about it. Thomas is the man I live with, and the man I love, and the man I met after my year in the mountains, when I enrolled in medical school, and now we have arranged, by the most persistent and elaborate of plans and pressure, to intern together at this large teaching hospital in this southern town where Monroe still works, though I did not know it when we got the assignment.

But I talked to Thomas about going to see Monroe, and confronting him, and asked if he'd like to come with me, and he said he would do whatever I thought was right, be there, or not, and I decided he should stay out of it, and we talked about that, and he suggested that confrontation was not best, but that I should call him, and set up a mannerly, sophisticated lunch, and just talk. Just give the meeting the opportunity to be civil, and for peace to be made.

But I want more than that. I still, after all these years, want something back. I do. It's wrong. Probably, it's wrong. Page said I've changed, and that I'm tougher now, and she likes that, but she's wrong, too. I'm not tougher. Not like she thinks. I'm softer. I'm softer to the people I love, warmer and softer and deeper with them than ever.

But I'm tougher about bad people, and I can recognize them faster, and I can get away from them faster, and I can tell them, directly looking them in the eye, if I have to go that far, to bug off, stay out of my life, I don't need you, I don't need anyone who makes my life more difficult than it's been, more trouble than it's been, though, in truth, I've had a wonderful life, and I know it, but I've also taught myself how to say the word, no, and I use it.

It's not that Monroe is a bad person. I actually did not mean to include him in that list. Monroe is a good person. He is. But he's scared of something, and confused, and I don't know what it is, and I don't care now, and won't spend my time thinking about it, but he's not a bad person. Not really.

But something's gone wrong with him, and just the vision of him with this woman, in short shorts and an ankle bracelet and high heels, tells me he's not the man I married, and that he's followed some part of himself too far, followed something somewhere, for what reason, I do not know, but I wonder how long he'll be with this woman. Surely, he won't stay with her long. Surely, he's not really interested in her. He can't be interested in a woman like her. Not the man I married. Not even the man I left. Not even the way he was by the time I had to leave. But I do wonder about it.

I'm only thinking about these things, and him, lately because I so unexpectedly saw him, and I will be talking to him soon, and that's the only reason he's in my thoughts, because I have spent four mind-boggling, fatiguing, heady, and happy years now, getting through med school, and living, the last two of them, with Thomas, the love of my life, a man so much like me, it's scary, but wonderful, scary because it's too good to believe, but wonderful because it's true, but still there it is. There he is. There's Monroe.

I must see him because I want to close it. I want the closure of that part of my life, and it can never be, without one last meeting, one last, truth-filled, reason-filled, dead-on reckoning.

I'll be nice about it, though. I can. I can be nice with him, and forgive him, because my life is good, and I am grateful for that.

chapter 40

I PHONED MONROE. HE did not answer. I called at night, and during the day, and he's never there. I know he works in the trauma unit, but I won't go there. It would be awkward. Thomas says it's a sign, this inability to reach him, and that I should forget the whole thing.

Thomas knows me well, and he smiled, and then laughed, after he said that, because he knew I would go anyway, hard-headed and determined as I am, and so I drove to Monroe's house.

This was not as easy as merely deciding to do it. It was the difference between understanding the forces of nature, at a distance, in the same way I had understood storms and floods and rain, and then actually feeling the earth tremble.

I drove to his house, and I looked at the number, and I stopped my car, but he was not home, or at least, there was no vehicle in his driveway, and just before I drove off, I noticed movement above me.

On the roof of his house was a teenaged girl, not the woman from the mall, and this girl was in cowboy clothes, sitting on the ridge, two stories and a steep pitched roof from the ground, with her elbows on her knees, and her chin resting in her hands, as relaxed and unconcerned, and at ease, as if she'd been on the floor, watching TV, and I thought, oh no, oh gosh, this is too much, this cannot be.

It could not be, because on one of the worst days of my life, when Monroe and I lived in Maine, and he had me out there, in the middle of nowhere, isolated from everything and everyone but him, and I was going mad, trying to understand why we'd moved up there, and why he'd changed so much, and in my confusion, trying to figure out what he wanted from me, and trying, if you can believe it, if anyone could believe it, after it's over, trying to actually *be* whatever it was he wanted, and one day, I thought I was going to split open, or scream, and I was not the kind of woman who screamed, and I went outside, and without planning to, climbed onto the shed roof, attached to the enormous, high dairy barn, and then me, scared of heights, me, scrambled up the old wood shingles of the steeper roof, to the ridge, and clung there, out on the edge, holding on as tightly as I could, afraid to move, unable to get down, and not going to jump.

I was not going to jump. I had not climbed up there for that. I climbed up, I suppose, to be away from him, from everything, to see better, to be able to breathe easier, to get above it all, anything you can imagine, but not to jump.

After some time, Monroe came out, and immediately, as if I'd given a signal, which I had not, looked up, and saw me, and climbed after me, and guided me down, and took me inside, and laid me on the bed, and made love to me.

It was strange lovemaking. It was tender, and I

cried while we made love, as quietly as I could, but it was sweet, and it was tender, and it was also horrible, because I did not want him to lead me down, and I did not want him to take me back inside, and I did not want him to make love to me. But I did. I did want him to, and I did not. I did not.

I was a mess back then, and I was as, yes, and as, no, as those earrings Page had sent me that I sometimes wore when I felt loose and happy, because one earring said, DO IT, and the other, said, DON'T DO IT. That was me. The funny me. But it wasn't funny. It was awful.

This cowgirl, on the roof of this house, was nothing like me, nothing at all, in relation to her feeling about heights, because after she watched me, watching her, she stood up, cleanly, and perfectly balanced, and then ran, mind you, ran down the steep roof, full speed, until she landed against the dormer outcropping, and swung around it and through the window as if it were nothing.

I suspected she might be coming to talk to me, and I waited. She sauntered toward the car, and I nodded at her, and she sat against the curb, and stared at me, and I held steady, certainly not going to be the one who broke and ran first, and finally she approached, and looked me over, and then said, in this bizarre, cowgirl-from-TV-land twang, Lady, if'n you looking for dance hall work, we ain't hiring.

And I laughed, because it was so fresh, and I thought she was the cutest little girl I'd seen in a long time, and I liked her, and I said, using my best cowgirl twang myself, well, ma'am, I ain't a lookin for dance hall work, but I was a-lookin for that fellow that owned the saloon.

And that stopped her for a moment, and then she

asked, in her natural voice, if I were looking for Monroe, and I said, yes, and she said, he was not there, and would not be back until late, and might be going out of town the next day, and the way she said it, had authority to it, some knowledge and certainty and possessiveness, even, that revealed to me there was more than a casual relationship here, and that what existed was intimate, and so I asked her, knowing, now, how to ask what I want to know, and having learned not to be too dignified, or too reserved, to do it, I asked her, if she lived with him.

No, she said, but I am his gal.

When she told me that, the affection I had initially felt for this girl went deeper and I loved her, then, in a sadly compassionate way, and I nodded, yes, I understand.

I only nodded to her, because though feeling deeply for her, the humor and the exotic and curious edge of knowing my ex-husband and this teenaged cowgirl were lovers suddenly fell flat, and we looked at each other, and I debated, quite consciously, how to give this girl advice, how to talk to her, how to let her know the things I now knew.

I thought of ways to begin the sentence, to start the conversation, to find a common ground on which we could stand, bonded not only by this same man, but as women, as mother and daughter, as sisters, as older and younger riders of the hills and prairies and bluffs of the West, in her parlance, and I said nothing.

Something was happening here, that did not concern me anymore. I was over here. She was over there. I had made the journey, and worked hard, and learned, and she would have to do the same. It is true, there are things people can tell you, but mostly you will have to learn them for yourself.

Who am I to deny anyone her happiness, for however long it will last, and who am I to take upon myself the coldness of presumption, of predicting and judging what will come in another person's life, or of secretly desiring vengeance on anyone, anywhere, when my life has grown to where it is now, where I am loved, and I am rich, and I am safe within myself, when I never was before, and so, I said nothing, but I looked her straight in the eye.

I saw her innocence, and her strength, and I knew she would be all right, and so I said nothing, but I wished her, with all my heart, that everything good that can happen to a person would happen to her, and just before I drove away, I almost said, happy trails, little girl, happy trails to you, but I kept quiet, and gave her the truest and warmest smile I could find within me, and she smiled at me, as if she knew more than the cowgirl act, and the twang, and the dance hall malarkey could disguise.

Then, she did something unexpected, and forever endearing. She reached to me, and patted me on the arm, and her hand was warm, and she held me, a long time, as if *she* were consoling *me*, as if I were the one who needed it, as if she had read me, as thoroughly, and as truly, as I had her.

I drove off then, having finally put to rest all those years, without even seeing Monroe, having closed it, then, like smoothing the sheets of a bed unmade for too long, tightening the blankets, smoothing the spread, and tucking it against the pillows, and running my hand across the unwrinkled expanse of order, and renewal, and faith.

41

RONNIE AND MONROE LEFT town a few days later. As they rolled down the street early that morning, Ronnie saw a group of animals gathered in a yard around the base of a tree.

"Look," she said, "there they are again."

"Who?" he asked, and looked as quickly as he could, but he did not see them.

"It's those animals again. I swear, they were looking at me. When we drove by, they turned their heads and were looking right at me."

Monroe patted her on the leg, and then checked the air conditioning level in the car.

"They looked worried about something."

"What's there to be worried about?" he asked.

They drove across the urban plains of central North Carolina, the remnants of what had been a new world to the Germans and the English who long ago settled there.

They drove into the foothills, and saw ahead of them, at the horizon, at the limits of physiological sight, the Blue Ridge Mountains.

"Gosh, I'm happy," Ronnie said.

"Me, too."

Had their eyes been distressed, they might not have seen that far. People whose eyes were afflicted, who had, for instance, strabismus, or eyes that turned inward, saw a world painted entirely different. Blows to the head, or psychic disturbances, often resulted in this type of malpositioning of the eye.

"I love you," Ronnie said.

"And I love you," Monroe told her.

The position of the eye, and its relation to its center, and to the flow of blood from the heart, all contribute to how one views the world. Some people's eyes float about, and they do not interpret life the way another might. Some people see spots, or specks. These are normal occurrences, if temporary, and are the result of the rush of blood through the corpuscles within the retina. That rush of blood, and the intensity of the spots, and the disturbance of the vision, are related to the speed and passion at which the heart itself beats, and thus, the illusions are tied to the heart in a way that a purely physical examination might not reveal.

"Tell me one of your stories," Ronnie said.

The mountains into which they climbed were settled centuries earlier, first by the Cherokee Indians and then by the Highlanders and Crofters from Scotland, a people banished and oppressed and misunderstood, who made the long journey into the remote valleys and windblown peaks, where, on any bright day, they could see into the distance. Vision was restored. Dreams began again.

"About what?" Monroe asked.

As they drove, they climbed the long, steep hill up Interstate 40, past Black Mountain, past Asheville.

Going down the other side, trucks geared and braked and tried to control themselves. There were sandtrap turnouts if they went too fast, if their brakes failed, if they could not stop themselves for whatever reason.

"I don't know. Stuff from the hospital."

Thirty miles to the northwest, up a winding dirt road that would never know the inhuman dimensions and urgency of the interstate, was the road to Katy's uncle's house. Along this road, dust, soft as rabbit's fur, sifted into the air, and deer, with lips as tender and smooth as velvet, quietly waited in the shadows.

"You mean funny stuff?"

"Yes."

When the human eye focuses on something unusually bright, such as the sun, or an incandescent bulb, blaring irreducibly, it appears that what one is seeing is surrounded by colored rings, often blue inside, and red on the outside. These colors are actually the tissue of the lens, and of the cornea, and are always there, but not ordinarily visible.

"Well, there was one man, a really funny case, who came in not long ago. He thought he'd gotten pregnant."

"Oh, great," Ronnie said, and laughed and grabbed Monroe's arm in delight. "Tell me that one."

A black eye is a common trauma. The old story of running into the door, used by women ever since the invention of the door, is no longer believed. What is not as commonly known is that the black eye can foretell a more serious condition.

"Well, this man walked in, and he was upset, and hyperventilating, and disoriented, and we got him calmed down, and finally, after talking and talking to him, and piecing together these bits of story, told out of sequence, we figured out he believed he'd just been impregnated.

"After a while, talking to this man, I got a group together, and drew him out, because it was turning into such a good story, I wanted to share it with a couple of my friends, and eventually, the man told us his theory on modern women."

"What was it?" Ronnie asked.

Pink eye, a problem decades ago, is not serious anymore, but problems with the tear ducts still exist. Tears come from the gland known as the lacrimal, and from this, six or so tiny tubes carry the tears to the eyes. There is also the nasal duct, which carries fluid from the eyes, to the nose, and therefore, when a person cries, his or her nose often runs simultaneously. A person whose ducts are blocked, and who needs to cry, who wants to cry, who deserves to cry, and cannot, must submit to surgical remedy.

"This man's theory was that women nowadays had such powerful orgasms, that they had begun to ejaculate their eggs out of their bodies, and into the men. The guy who'd been telling us this came in just after he said his girlfriend had made love to him, and had been on top, and he was quite certain that, due to the force of her orgasm, and the fact that she'd been on top, and the pull of gravity downward into him, he had become impregnated."

"Oh, gosh," Ronnie said, and laughed. "I love it. I love things like that. I want you to tell me all kinds of stuff like that."

"Yes. Maybe later," he said. "Right now, baby, my sweetheart, my girl of my dreams," he said, and drew her to him, "let's drive."

They drove on. They crossed the mountains, and started through the cuts of geologic history that this high-speed road had carved through these ancient hills with explosive clarity.

As they drove, Monroe received a fleeting and uneasy vision of himself and Katy driving up to Maine after he'd left school. For a moment, it seemed like the same thing, the same feeling, the same excitement, the same freshness, the same effortless companionship and sense of adventure that he'd felt as he and Katy drove north, not west, but north, into the cold unknown, which, in itself, had been part of the challenge and adventure, but the more he thought about it, the more he realized it was not the same.

It was not merely that they were going west and not north, and therefore following the historically correct route to renewal and reward. It was simply that this was Ronnie, and not Katy, and they were different people, different women, and he'd learned enough, he was sure, he hoped, anyway, he certainly hoped, to have chosen the right one this time, who meant it when she said, I'm yours.

The vision receded. Time passed. Monroe did not speak. He was glad for the vision, and pleased he'd understood the difference.

Ronnie watched him. He seemed, to her, lost in thought, and she wanted to know what it was to make contact, to know where he was, and where she was. She wanted to talk to him about something she'd been thinking about, and had wanted to talk about for some time. She chose this moment, then, to try.

"Can I ask you one more thing?" she said.

"Sure."

"Do you think we'll ever have children?"

"Why?"

"Because I love children. And I'd like to have some. I'd like to have your child. Our child."

Monroe did not answer right away. Ronnie watched his face, and waited.

"No," he said, when he finally spoke.

"No? But, I mean . . . don't most women . . . I mean, didn't Katy want children?"

"She wanted what I wanted."

"Oh."

The presbyopic eyes had problems different from the anastigmatic eye or the myopic. The presbyopic eye was formed by a loss of elasticity in the lens. This creates a person who cannot focus well, who cannot see what he is supposed to see when he looks up from something close at hand to something further away. Practically everyone over the age of forty-five becomes presbyopic.

"Could a woman do that? Really?" Ronnie asked.

"What?"

"Get a man pregnant."

"No. Not literally."

"I didn't think so."

"Of course, things are changing. There's a case being talked about, that a colleague told me—it's purely anecdotal at this point—that concerns a woman whose vestigial equivalent of what still exists on the man was found to be frighteningly similar in size and development."

"What are you talking about?"

"Nothing," he said, and laughed. "It was a joke. Just something I thought of."

Ronnie studied his face, and his laughter, and then, she laughed, too, not because she understood, but because she loved him, and wanted to share in this fun, in whatever it was that gave him such delight.

"You're terrific," she said. "Dr. Terrific, that's who you are."

After that, she said nothing, because she knew that, in the silence, the love she had for him would speak for itself.

Letting the love speak for itself was one of the ways women used to be. Then they changed. Now it was starting to happen again. Maybe it would work better this time. Maybe everyone had learned enough by now.

"You're perfect," he said. "You're just the most perfect woman on earth," he told her.

This was a nice thing to hear, and it would be wonderful if it were true. Wouldn't it?

Books in the
HARVEST AMERICAN WRITING SERIES

The Choiring of the Trees
Donald Harington

Let the Dead Bury Their Dead
Randall Kenan

Taller Women: A Cautionary Tale
Lawrence Naumoff

Patchwork
Karen Osborn

Marbles
Oxford Stroud

Blue Glass
Sandra Tyler